UNIVERSAL PICTURES PRESENTS AN EDWARD R. PRESSMAN AND CAPCOM CO., LTD. PRODUCTION JEAN-CLAUDE VAN DAMME   RAUL JULIA "STREET FIGHTER"

MING-NA WEN   DAMIAN CHAPA   KYLIE MINOGUE AND WES STUDI   MUSIC BY GRAEME REVELL   EXECUTIVE MUSIC PRODUCER BARRY LEVINE   LINE PRODUCER GRANT HILL   ASSOCIATE PRODUCERS AKIO SAKAI   KENICHI IMAI   HIROSHI NOZAKI

COSTUMES DESIGNED BY MARILYN VANCE   COSTUME DESIGNER DEBORAH LA GORCE KRAMER   FILM EDITORS DOV HOENIG A.C.E.   ANTHONY REDMAN A.C.E.   PRODUCTION DESIGNER WILLIAM CREBER   DIRECTOR OF PHOTOGRAPHY WILLIAM A. FRAKER A.S.C.

EXECUTIVE PRODUCERS TIM ZINNEMANN   JUN AIDA   SASHA HARARI   BASED ON THE CAPCOM VIDEO GAME "STREET FIGHTER II"   PRODUCED BY EDWARD R. PRESSMAN AND KENZO TSUJIMOTO   WRITTEN AND DIRECTED BY STEVEN E. DE SOUZA

CAPCOM   PG-13 PARENTS STRONGLY CAUTIONED   Some Material May be Inappropriate for Children Under 13   DIGITAL dts SOUND   STREET FIGHTER AND STREET FIGHTER CHARACTERS ™ & © CAPCOM CO., LTD.   A UNIVERSAL RELEASE   UNIVERSAL   AN MCA COMPANY

SOUNDTRACK ALBUM ON PRIORITY RECORDS FEATURING NEW SONGS FROM ICE CUBE · CRAIG MACK · THE PHARCYDE · DEION SANDERS & HAMMER · NAS/RAS KASS/SAEFIR · LL COOL J · MAS · AND MORE

By Todd Strasser
Based on the screenplay by Steven E. de Souza

B▦XTREE

Published in Great Britain in 1995 by Boxtree Limited,
Broadwall House, 21 Broadwall, London SE1 9PL.

First published in the United States in 1994 by Newmarket Press, 18 East 48th
Street, New York, New York 10017.

Printed by Cox and Wyman, Reading, Berkshire.

ISBN 0 7522 0659 1

10 9 8 7 6 5 4 3 2 1

A CIP catalogue entry for this book is available from the British Library.

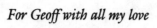
For Geoff with all my love

One

Deep in the misty jungles of the Shadaloo delta, an ancient stone temple stood hidden among the tropical trees and vines. Snakes slithered through the loose, moss-covered stones that had once been monuments to long-forgotten deities. Screeching monkeys scampered playfully up the crumbling stone steps, and small Asian deer grazed quietly among the fallen rocks that had once been the temple's stone walls. It was a place that appeared to be empty and deserted.

But it was not what it seemed.

For months the small Asian country of Shadaloo had been engulfed by a vicious civil war between the government and the forces of a maniacal warlord who called himself General M. Bison. Fueled with almost limitless funds from drug running, extortion, and gambling, the renegade general had waged the war with sophisticated weapons purchased from Libya, Iraq, and any other nation willing to sell.

But Bison was no petty crook. He had no intention of stopping until he ruled not only Shadaloo, but also all of Southeast Asia, and from there, the world.

Hidden deep under that ancient temple was an ultra-modern fortress. There Bison sat at his desk, a thick slab of video monitors, consoles, and other electronic wizardry that floated on a platform in midair. Looking like a small, convertible flying saucer, the desk hovered about the Bison command center with the help of superconductivty.

Bison was a large man with slicked-back black hair and the round, fiendish eyes of a venomous snake. He wore a high-peaked green military cap with a silver insignia of a winged skull pinned to it. This morbid image was Bison's logo and was on everything he touched, from the uniforms of his soldiers to the curtains in his private quaters. A long, gray-colored cape was held in place by a similarly shaped clasp. Beneath the cape was a red body suit of woven body armor that not only protected him but also contained a state-of-the-art life support system. His hands were encased in red gloves of the same material.

Before him spread his vast hi-tech electronic headquarters, shaped much like a NASA command center. Below were rows of computerized battle consoles, their screens bright with graphs, war maps, and scenes of actual fighting in other parts of Shadaloo. Dozens of technicians monitored the consoles, while on crisscrossing catwalks above, Bison troopers wearing red helmets and chrome face guards patrolled.

Dominating the entire room was a bank of video monitors on the wall above the consoles and across from Bison's desk. On these monitors Bison watched comfortably as his war waged on.

At that moment Bison was paying no attention to the scenes of mayhem and destruction that played on the monitors like two dozen different horror movies. Instead, his attention was turned to a dark-haired man with intelligent eyes who was wearing the white coat of a scientist. The man's hands and feet were bound by shackles, and a heavy steel ring hung around his neck. A fearsome guard armed with an automatic rifle stood behind him.

"So, Dr. Dhalsim, what progress have you made?" Bison asked, pretending to wear a benign smile.

"Some," the older man replied, making no attempt to hide the scorn in his voice.

"Only *some*?" Bison's eyebrows rose and his eyes narrowed. "I expect your genetic mutation device to be working by tonight."

"But that isn't enough time," Dhalsim said.

"I say it is," Bison replied, his face darkening. "If it isn't, I will make sure that you die a slow and exquisitely painful death."

Dhalsim nodded. Ever since he was kidnapped by Bison's men in Stockholm and brought to this madhouse, he had endured such threats. The problem was, they weren't idle. He had seen Bison have men killed for far less.

The familiar Global News Television jingle floated across the room from the bank of video monitors. Bison quickly spun around in his seat to watch as videos of his very own tanks were shown rumbling across scorched, war-torn fields and the words CRISIS IN SHADALOO flashed onto the screen.

Immediately forgetting the recalcitrant Dr. Dhalsim, Bison smiled, delighted that once again he was dominating world news. He was even more delighted when the video cut to his favorite GNT reporter, the young, attractive, and curvaceous Chun-Li Zang.

Bison quickly pressed a TV remote and the pretty black-haired reporter filled every screen on the wall. She was wearing an olive-colored photographer's vest over a white blouse and light tan slacks. The bangs of her straight black hair stopped just above her eyes.

"Allied Nations forces are consolidating their hold on Shadaloo City today," Chun-Li reported, holding a microphone and gesturing to lines of soldiers marching past her, wearing the robin's egg blue berets and gray and blue camouflage uniforms that earmarked the AN forces. "This concludes a night of skirmishing that secured this key Southeast Asian port. But these soldiers aren't celebrating just yet. They know that defeating the ragtag city militia is one thing. But defeating the heavily armed forces of General M. Bison is quite another."

Bison smiled to himself. Truer words had rarely been spoken.

"It's only been twenty-four hours since the dangerously unpredictable warlord seized sixty-three unarmed Allied Nations relief workers from a village north of here," Chun-Li continued. "The self-styled general's ransom demand is an astounding twenty billion dollars. Meanwhile, at this time, the location of the sixty-three hostages remains unknown."

To you, my dear, Bison thought with a smile, gazing down at a massive steel door in the center of the command room. Beneath that door, on the floor below, the hostages huddled in the dark in a pitlike metal dungeon.

"The AN forces know that in Bison they are facing a power-mad dictator," the young reporter continued, "a dictator whose drug money has equipped his army with hi-tech weaponry that some intelligence experts fear is equal to anything in the industrialized world."

Bison shook his head. Here she was wrong. Not equal to, but far *beyond* anything in the industrialized world, thanks to his friend Dr. Dhalsim.

"Of the fifteen Allied Nations troops assigned to protect the missing relief workers, twelve are confirmed dead and three are missing," Chun-Li added.

Bison glanced to his right, where the three AN soldiers now stood with hoods covering their heads and their hands tied behind their backs. They were surrounded by four heavily armed guards carrying black automatic rifles with shiny bayonets. The guards wore the trademark red uniforms of the Armies of Bison. Their heads were covered by deep-red helmets, and their faces were obscured by shiny chrome face masks.

The sight and sound of his favorite reporter talking about his latest conquest filled the rebel leader with a lust for violence. He stood up.

Immediately his personal bodyguard, a giant of a man named Zangief, stepped out of the shadows. The bodyguard had a thick black beard. His hair was shaved into a Mohawk. He had barely finished the third grade and his education since then consisted of one idea: Bison was his God.

"Remove my cape," Bison ordered. "Yes, sir." Zangief immediately drew the cape back from his master's shoulders. Bison stretched his arms and pulled his hands into fists. A yearning for violence flooded through his veins. It was time. He needed to find the right specimen for his greatest experiment ever—the specimen who, when treated by Dr. Dhalsim, would become the greatest killer who ever walked the earth.

Bison nodded at the guards and gestured to one of the AN soldiers. "Untie him."

The guards untied the soldier's hands and pulled the black hood off his head. The soldier looked around and blinked, clearly disoriented.

"You came from across the world to fight me, soldier," Bison said, clenching and unclenching his fists. "Now, finally, you have your chance."

The soldier focused on him and felt the prickly nudge of the bayonets behind him. Realizing that he was facing the rebel leader himself, the man lunged forward.

His attack was so feeble that Bison almost smiled. He quickly sidestepped the man, tripped him, and drove an elbow into his kidney.

Splat! The man crashed to the floor, writhing for a moment in agony before losing consciousness.

"Pathetic," Bison muttered. The experience had done nothing to satisfy his thirst for violence or his need for an appropriate guinea pig. He turned to the next man. "Your turn."

This AN soldier launched himself into the air, throwing a jabbing kick at Bison's face. It was an improvement, but just barely. Bison easily blocked the kick and upended the man with a kick of his own.

Thunk! The man's head smacked the floor. Bison heard the sickening sound of bones cracking and smiled. The man fell into an unconscious heap.

Bison shook his head in disgust. It might be harder to find his warrior than he'd thought. Rather than fight the remaining AN soldier, he turned back to the bank of video monitors. Still on the air, Chun-Li was gesturing toward an armored vehicle pulling up behind her. A tall, powerfully built AN colonel hopped out of the vehicle and started walking toward her, wearing a light blue beret and camouflage uniform. He had short blond hair and a chiseled, handsome face with penetrating blue eyes and a firm, hard jaw.

"I think I see the AN commander coming this way," Chun-Li said, moving quickly toward him. "I'll try to get a few words with him."

The pretty young reporter stuck her microphone in his face. The colonel continued to walk.

"Colonel Guile," she said, "may we talk to you?"

"No."

Bison watched on the screen as Guile continued past the reporter, so unlike the normally publicity-hungry types who craved the world's audience. He was followed by a pretty young British woman whose pigtails were pinned up under her AN beret. There was a faded combat scar on her cheek. Her name was Cammy. She and a tall, Native American soldier named T. Hawk were Colonel Guile's aides. T. Hawk walked beside Cammy, his head wrapped with gauze from a recent wound.

While Chun-Li scurried after Guile on the monitor, Bison turned to the sole remaining AN prisoner—a captain. As the hood was pulled from his head, the officer blinked and focused more quickly than his companions had. He was a striking Brazilian man with short black hair and an athletic build. His name was Carlos Blanka.

Sensing instantly what he was up against, Blanka struck a fighting stance. A dozen feet away, Bison smiled with perverse pleasure and got into a stance of his own. It was clear that this AN officer knew how to fight.

"Finally," he said, "a workout."

The Bison guards backed away as the two men circled each other, neither falling for the other's feints. Meanwhile, the broadcast continued to blare from the opposite wall of the command post.

"Colonel," Chun-Li said with a gasp, catching up to Guile, "don't you want to speak to the world audience?"

Colonel Guile stopped and glared at her, seemingly unaware that he was being captured live for a worldwide audience. "Why? The world chickened out in Bosnia and Rwanda. I wouldn't talk to them on a bet."

The commander started to turn away, but then stopped and turned back to the camera. "But I do want to speak to someone: that wannabe dictator called General Bison."

In the command post, Bison was so surprised to hear himself addressed by Guile that he turned to look at the screen. Seeing an opportunity, Carlos Blanka swung hard.

Wham! He caught Bison in the jaw, knocking the creep backward.

Holding his jaw with one hand, Bison pointed at the soldiers and screamed at his men. "Hold him!" Then he turned back to the screen.

On the television, Colonel Guile grabbed the mike out of Chun-Li's hand and glared into the camera. "I know you like to look at yourself on television, you twisted clown, so look at this!" Guile made a well-known gesture with his hand.

Bison felt himself fill with rage. He spun around and yelled at a dark-skinned man bent over a complicated-looking electronics console. "Dee Jay, break in! Now!"

Dee Jay was an expert electronics technician, and his fingers raced over the electronic control board like a concert pianist typing instructions.

"Satellite in range!" he called out. "We're riding the beam."

High above them, atop the temple ruins, a sophisticated satellite dish suddenly rose through the rocks, scaring off the monkeys and birds. As the dish tilted skyward, a high-pitched whine burst from it.

Down below, in the command center, Bison turned to Blanka and narrowed his eyes. He stepped toward him and reached toward the soldier's neck. Blanka moved to defend himself, but half a dozen of Bison's men poked their bayonets menacingly at him. Blanka put his hands down.

Bison didn't grab the man's throat. Instead, he reached into his shirt and pulled out his dog tags.

"Carlos Blanka," he read. Bison touched his sore jaw. "No one has drawn blood from me in many years, Carlos Blanka." Bison turned to his men. Here was a subject worthy of his plans. "Take him to the laboratory."

As the men led Blanka away, Zangief sidled up to his boss. "Dr. Dhalsim's laboratory?"

Bison nodded slowly. "Yes, I think Captain Blanka will make a very interesting . . . specimen."

Two

Many miles away, at the Allied Nations compound in Shadaloo City, Chun-Li Zang yanked her microphone back from Colonel Guile. Next time, she vowed to herself, she would wear a wireless mike that wouldn't be so easy to grab. She turned once again to face her camera crew. Her cameraman, a powerfully built African American named Balrog, focused the camera in on her. Balrog wore a green vest over a tight purple T-shirt. A gold earring glinted in his ear.

The sun was starting to set and the cameraman flicked on a small spotlight.

"Thank you, Colonel Guile," Chun-Li began, but she was abruptly cut short by a surprise announcement through her earphone from the tech person inside the GNT van. Quickly regaining her composure, the young reporter addressed the world audience. "I . . . I've just been informed that GNT has received a transmission . . . from General Bison himself! We'll go now live to the rebel warlord."

A few feet away, Guile smiled and turned to look at the small portable TV monitor Ms. Zang took her cues from. On the screen, Chun-Li dissolved into static and was then replaced by the image of the renegade general himself. This was just what Guile had hoped would happen.

Guile quickly turned to Cammy. "He took the bait. Trace that signal, STAT."

"But electronic warfare hasn't off-loaded," Cammy replied in her British accent.

Guile quickly looked around the AN compound, a group of buildings surrounded by a tall stone wall topped with barbed wire.

"Then commandeer something!" Guile barked. "Anything! Just move! We've got to get a read on that signal and trace it."

The only possibility was the blue and silver GNT news van parked in the courtyard next to the AN headquarters building. Cammy dashed toward it, with T. Hawk right behind. She yanked open the door and froze. Inside the van was the largest man she'd ever seen. His name was Edmund Honda, and Cammy guessed correctly that he must have been a sumo wrestler. Of course, the brightly colored Hawaiian shirt was sort of a giveaway, as was the huge submarine sandwich he was in the process of devouring while he worked the switchboard. His black hair was short except for a long black ponytail that hung down his back.

"Move aside!" Cammy ordered.

Honda looked at her like she was crazy. "I *am* aside."

Cammy saw his point. With Honda inside, there was barely any room for anyone else.

"Well, inhale!" Cammy yelled, and climbed into the van, followed by T. Hawk.

"What are you doing?" Honda asked.

"Taking over," T. Hawk informed him, and started to flick switches on the electronic video console.

Meanwhile, outside on the tiny monitor, Bison had begun to address the commander of the AN forces.

17

"Colonel Guile, why do you address a fellow warrior with such disrespect?"

Guile laughed. "Warrior? You? I've known tapeworms with more honor than you'll ever see. How many doctors and nurses have you killed this week, Bison? How many children have you orphaned? How many villages destroyed?"

Inside the GNT van, Cammy and T. Hawk were having problems tracking Bison's signal. Cammy leaned out of the van and motioned to Guile to stretch things out and keep Bison talking as long as possible.

On the monitor, Bison glowered at him. "You will choke on those words, Guile."

"Anytime, bozo," Guile taunted the man, hoping to keep him ranting and raving long enough for Cammy and T. Hawk to get a fix on his secret command post. "We'll go worldwide, just like now. The profits from the pay per view can go to the families of your victims."

On the screen, General Bison was momentarily distracted by a whispered warning from Dee Jay. He turned back to the monitors. "So you're tracing this. You think you're clever, Guile? Well, think about this. You have three days. If my twenty billion dollars is not delivered by then, the hostages will die. And the world will hold *you* responsible!"

In the background, Bison's men began to chant their leader's name. Sensing that they were about to be cut off, Guile spoke quickly. "You hostages—if you can hear me—we're coming. Charlie, hang on, buddy, we're on our way."

The monitor screen went to static. Guile felt his spirits fall. His closest friend, Carlos "Charlie" Blanka, had been assigned to lead the detail of AN soldiers whose job was to protect the civilian relief workers. When the relief workers were kidnapped, Charlie must have been taken into that sadist's hands.

The door of the GNT van swung open and Cammy and T. Hawk climbed out with dour expressions on their faces.

Cammy gave the colonel the bad news. "We couldn't trace the signal. Bison broke off too soon."

Guile shook his head angrily and stared at Chun-Li. "For a minute you were almost useful."

He turned and strode toward the AN headquarters. Chun-Li couldn't believe how unfriendly he'd been. She looked over at Cammy.

"He doesn't like women, does he?" she asked.

"Oh, no, ma'am," Cammy answered with all sincerity. "He likes women just fine. It's reporters he doesn't like. I assure you it's an equal opportunity dislike."

Cammy turned and jogged to catch up to Guile. Chun-Li followed her. The sun continued to fall, and it was almost dark now. Chun-Li had places to go, but not before she let the commander of the AN forces know that he wasn't going to get off easily. She ran ahead and stood in front of him, blocking his path.

"Colonel Guile," she said, trying to keep her anger from spilling into her words, "what makes you think you can behave like this?"

"I have my own army," Guile replied. "I can behave any way I want."

"And you like it, don't you?" Chun-Li's words reeked of sarcasm.

"Yeah, it's pretty cool." Guile knew how to dish it right back.

Chun-Li glared at him. "You better get used to me,

Colonel. I'm going to be here until the war is over."

"That's a good reason to get it over with as soon as possible," Guile replied, and turned to Cammy. "Lieutenant, make a note. End war as quickly as possible."

"Yes, sir." Cammy saluted with a slight smile.

Chun-Li was fuming. She was getting tired of this man, who was nearly as full of himself as that madman Bison. "You may find yourself amusing, Colonel, but I don't. The whole world is watching the events here in Shadaloo, and you have an obligation to—"

"My only obligation is to take this dictator Bison down so fast and so hard that the next dictator decides to get into a safer line of work," Guile shot back, cutting her short. "I don't have to give you interviews, sound bites, or the time of day."

Colonel Guile looked down at his watch. "And speaking of the time of day, this city is under curfew. You'd better get moving, miss. Press passes are invalid after dark."

"You can't do that!" Chun-Li said with a gasp.

"No?" Guile gave her a big smile and nodded toward the GNT van.

Chun-Li turned and felt her jaw drop. The van was being towed away by a military vehicle! Her cameraman Balrog and tech person Honda were running as fast as they could across the courtyard, chasing after it.

"Hey!" Chun-Li cried, dashing after them. "Wait!"

Guile and his aides watched them chase the van into the darkness. Guile shook his head and sighed. "The press. Can't live with 'em . . . . Can't put 'em in front of a firing squad."

The others chuckled. Guile knew it was important to

keep the facade and morale up. But the truth was, he was worried. He had fewer than seventy-two hours to find Bison's secret fortress and command post and save those hostages. He didn't doubt that if he was one minute late, Bison would have every last one of them slaughtered.

Three

The waterfront of the Port of Shadaloo was a dark, sinister place filled with dilapidated boats, flimsy piers, and stagnant water. Lining the shore were various warehouses and shacks where the affairs of the underworld were commonly transacted. During the day it bustled with legitimate activity, but at night it was a no-man's-land visited only by the most heavily armed and dangerous characters.

In the shadows under a dock, in a small rowboat "borrowed" for the occasion, Ken Masters and Ryu Hoshi huddled and waited. Ken, an American with light brown hair, wore a brown vest and green tie over a blue denim shirt. Ryu, a handsome young Asian man with black hair and dark eyes, wore a white jacket over a black shirt and carried a small backpack.

"I don't like this, man, I just don't like it," Ryu whispered. Water dripped from piers around them, and they could hear the scratching sounds of water rats going about their nightly business.

"Just chill, okay?" Ken whispered back. "Everything'll be fine."

"Man, if I had a dollar for every time you've said that," Ryu said.

"Yeah, I know," Ken replied. "You'd be rich. If that's

what you wanted, I don't know why you didn't just stay in Japan and work for your famous industrialist father."

"Because I'm not a company man," Ryu replied. "Neither are you."

"Right, we're just a couple of street fighters and con artists who somehow manage to stay one step ahead of the law," Ken said. "So the last thing I need is to listen to your complaints."

They heard the throaty grumble of an approaching AN patrol boat. A searchlight swept over them, and Ken and Ryu instinctively ducked. A second later a staticky voice coming through a loudspeaker split the night's silence: *"Attention: By order of Colonel Guile of the Allied Nations forces, there is a 7 p.m. curfew in effect for Shadaloo City. Violators will be arrested. Anyone resisting will be shot."*

As the patrol boat passed, the rowboat hidden under the pier bobbed up and down on the wake.

"Okay," Ken whispered, grabbing onto the pier, "time to bail."

Ken climbed out from under the pier. Ryu followed, clutching his canvas bag and shaking his head.

"Why are we here?" he whispered. "We were doing so well with the street fights in Manila."

"It was small change, Ryu," Ken reminded him. "Besides, you were in a rut. You kept winning."

"And this is a great improvement," Ryu said, shaking his head. "Now we're in the middle of a war zone."

"Plácido, amigo," Ken replied as he walked quickly toward a dark warehouse. "Our luck is about to change. By this time tomorrow we'll be on a plane, sipping champagne and eating caviar and counting our money. Trust me, we'll be out of here before the first shot gets fired."

"Drop your anchor!" the loudspeaker voice suddenly cracked through the damp night air. *"Prepare to be board-ed!"*

Startled, Ken and Ryu looked up. One hundred yards up the dark river, the patrol boat had pulled alongside a ragtag sailboat.

Pow! Pow! Someone on the sailboat started to shoot.

Ka-boom! The patrol boat immediately returned fire with its deck gun, ripping a huge hole in the sailboat's bow. Shattered pieces of wood, sails, and rope flew everywhere, and the sailboat quickly sank. Half a dozen men, apparently involved in *some* kind of illegal enterprise, dove into the water and started to swim for safety.

Ryu gave Ken a baleful look. "Before the first shot gets fired?"

"Hey, how was I to know?" Ken asked with a smirk. He stopped in the shadows next to a boarded-up door and knocked twice.

The door swung open and Ken and Ryu were yanked inside by muscular arms.

Bang! The door slammed shut behind them. Even before their eyes had a chance to adjust to the lights, massive hands patted them down, searching for weapons. The sounds of a loud, excited crowd reached their ears. As Ken's and Ryu's eyes adjusted, they found themselves at the edge of a crowd of nasty-looking hoods, seductively dressed women, and haggard gambling addicts pressing in toward a caged fighting ring. Clearly this was a violation of the AN curfew.

The scene was immediately familiar. The crowd was gambling on the lives of two fighters in the ring. Ryu took a closer look and realized the ring wasn't marked off with ropes, but with razor sharp concertina wire. This wasn't boxing, it was cage fighting, where anything was allowed and the only thing that mattered was outliving the opponent.

Ryu felt someone nudge him in the ribs. Turning, he found Ken winking at him.

"I know you love this stuff," Ken said, teasing him. "But we're here on business."

Ken started toward a stairs that led to an office above the fighting ring. Ryu followed.

"Okay, we're off the street," Ken said in a low voice to his pal as they started up the stairs. "Feel safe yet?"

Just then the crowd roared. Halfway up the stairs, Ryu turned and looked into the ring. A fighter stood there with his hands raised in triumph. Ryu noticed that the man was wearing a metal mask. The steel claw on his right hand was bloody. At his feet lay the loser, his neck twisted in a way that left no doubt. He was dead.

"Yeah," Ryu muttered. "Now I feel *real* safe."

At the top of the stairs they were stopped by yet another guard and again searched, as if they'd somehow miraculously acquired weapons on the way up. To Ryu it meant that the man they were seeing took no chances. He had a bad feeling about this, a *very* bad feeling.

They stepped into a smoke-filled room lit by dim lamps covered with sheer red material. The walls were decorated with gold and red oriental designs, and the floor was covered with oriental rugs. The room was filled with dangerous-looking thugs wearing jackets and ties. They might have been better dressed than the crowd below, but they were no less menacing.

From their midst stepped a tall man with a completely bald head. He wore a black eyepatch that only emphasized the cold glare of the remaining eye. His muscles bulged against the fabric of his shiny black suit. A blood-red tie hung from his neck.

Ken and Ryu both recognized him at once. His name was Viktor Sagat, and he was the head of the Shadaloo Tong, the highly organized and extremely vicious gang that virtually ruled the city.

"Good evening, gentlemen," Sagat said without offering his hand.

"Evening, Sagat," Ryu said, nodding down to the crowd around the caged ring. "That's quite a party. Didn't anyone tell you there's a curfew?"

"In Shadaloo no one tells me anything," Sagat replied coldly. "May I offer you a drink?"

"Let's skip the Miss Manners routine and get down to business," Ken said. "You got the hundred K?"

Sagat turned and snapped his fingers. One of his men came forward with an attaché case and opened it. Inside was $100,000 in American bills. Ryu felt his eyes widen slightly. Ken reached toward the money, but the man snapped the attaché case shut before he could touch it.

"Where are the weapons?" Sagat asked.

Ken glanced at the room full of heavies. "They're hidden . . . not far from here."

Ryu knew that was his cue. He pulled a small walkie-talkie out of his bag. "When we get outside with our money, we'll call you on this and tell you where your guns are."

Sagat gave them a nasty smile. "You two are overly cautious."

"Yeah, we even sleep with seat belts," Ken said, nodding at the attaché case. "Now how about it?"

Sagat nodded, and the briefcase was handed over to Ken. The tall man with the eyepatch turned away.

"Hey," Ryu said, holding out the walkie-talkie. "Don't you want this?"

Sagat stopped and turned to them. "I don't need you to tell me that the truck with the weapons is on the pier behind the Malpeza Brewery. One of my men followed you yesterday when you hid them. In fact, my men have already unloaded the truck and brought the weapons here."

Ryu and Ken glanced at each other out of the corners of their eyes. Ryu felt a bolt of nervousness shoot through him and knot in his stomach. This was bad news, *very* bad news.

Now four men carrying complex-looking automatic rifles stepped out of the shadows. They jammed ammo clips in and aimed the guns at Ken and Ryu.

Ryu glanced at Ken. "Everything'll be fine, huh?"

"Hey," Ken replied with a shrug, "I do the best I can. That's all I can do."

Ryu swallowed and swore he'd never listen to Ken again, *if* he lived through this. Meanwhile, Sagat studied them.

"What's wrong, gentlemen?" he asked with a sinister smile. "Surely you're not afraid of your own weapons? After all, you were brave enough to steal them from the Pentagon. You told me so yourself. Two heroes brave enough to rob the American military surely cannot fear a handful of simple men from the Shadaloo Tong."

Sagat smiled at his men and nodded.

Ken and Ryu shut their eyes.

Sagat's men squeezed the triggers of the guns.

Bam! Bam! Bam! Bam! Bam!

The automatic rifles opened fire.

Ken and Ryu felt the bullets hit them . . .

And bounce off.

They were harmless yellow Nerf projectiles.

The guns were nothing but fancy toys, bought from a manufacturer in Hong Kong. Just another one of Ken's great ideas for scamming the bad guys.

Never again . . . Ryu told himself.

"Toys!" Sagat shouted furiously at them. "You tried to sell me toys! Did you think you were dealing with a fool?"

Ryu shot Ken a look. "I'm beginning to."

"Sagat, you have to have a sense of humor about these things," Ken said, scrambling to talk his way out of this. He held out the attaché case. "Okay, here's your money. We'll just take our toys back and—"

Sagat glared at him. Ken knew he had to change gears.

"Okay, keep the money *and* the toys," he said. "Maybe you guys have kids. They love stuff like this. By the way, we also have a connection for video games—"

"I like my games live," Sagat spit ominously. "And in living color. Make that . . . dying color."

Sagat turned and nodded at his men. The next thing Ryu knew, half a dozen of the biggest, meanest-looking thugs he'd ever seen were charging toward him, pulling knives, blackjacks, and nunchucks.

And none of *those* weapons looked like toys.

Four

Ken threw the attaché case into one man's face, then leaped into the air and reverse-roundhoused a second in the head.

"Ahhhh!" The man went flying backward and smashed into a dresser.

Wham! Pow! Crash! Ryu went into an offensive crouch and took out three thugs with a combination of vicious kicks and jabs. Ken brought another down with a jarring uppercut. Six, seven, eight men went down . . . but more kept coming.

"Ooof! Unh! Ahhhh!" Ken and Ryu fought valiantly, but the sheer mass of the thugs overwhelmed them. Finally they were tackled and thrown down.

Click! Click! Cocked pistols were pressed hard against their temples.

Standing among the prostrate bodies of his groaning men, Sagat crossed his arms and nodded gravely at the two street fighters.

"Interesting," he said with a bemused smile. "You two can fight. You're not all talk after all."

"I could have told you that," Ryu said.

"Bring them to their feet and follow me," Sagat ordered his men.

With the cold, hard barrels of the pistols pressed firmly against their heads, Ken and Ryu were yanked to their feet and led out of the office and down the stairs. The crowd of cutthroats and gamblers parted as Sagat marched up to the caged ring and turned toward the street fighters.

"Which of you is the better fighter?" the Shadaloo Tong leader asked.

Ken and Ryu both started to answer at the same time, but before they finished, a brutal-looking man climbed into the ring. His black hair was pulled back into a long, braided ponytail. Naked to the waist, muscles bulging, he wore a steel face mask and black matador's pants lined with silver designs. In the audience, dozens of women began to shout and wave signs.

"Must be a popular guy with the ladies," Ken whispered to Ryu.

Ryu nodded silently. Now he saw that attached to the fighter's right hand was a razor-sharp claw with blades extending at least a foot. Tattooed across his chest was a huge snake—the trademark of the Shadaloo Tong. This, Ryu realized, was the same fighter who had killed a man in the ring earlier that evening.

"So?" Sagat asked. "Have you made up your mind?"

Ken and Ryu quickly pointed at each other and said at the same time, "*He's* the better fighter."

Sagat smirked and drew a coin from his pocket. He flipped in the air, inspected it, and pointed at Ryu. Then to the crowd he announced, "The challenger, Ryu. The defender, my champion, Vega!"

The crowd launched into a fury of betting. In the ring, Vega removed the mask and bowed to the crowd. The women screamed with joy. Under the mask, he was surprisingly handsome, but his eyes were chillingly dead.

Hands reached toward Ryu and started to rip his jacket and shirt off. He felt sick inside. Ken leaned toward him.

"Don't worry, the guy's wearing knickers," he whispered. "He must be a wuss."

"Those are matador pants," Ryu replied. "Those guys kill raging bulls with swords."

"Oh, well, in that case, just remember everything I taught you," Ken whispered.

"That'll last me about ten seconds," Ryu whispered back.

He was pushed toward the ring and ducked under the wires. A gaudily painted woman offered him a machete.

Ryu weighed the large knife in his hand and gazed across the ring at Vega and the razor-sharp claw. An idea quickly formed in his head. He wouldn't stand a chance against that claw, but maybe he could shame Vega into not using it.

Ryu turned and hurled the machete into one of the wooden posts holding up the cage. Then he turned back to Vega and presented his bare hands, palms up.

Across the ring, Vega scowled. He knew Ryu was daring him to fight without weapons. He wouldn't have done it, but in front of the crowd and all his fans, he couldn't back down. He slowly removed the stainless-steel claw. Ryu felt a little better. His gamble had paid off.

Standing beside the ring with Ken, Sagat nodded in approval. "Good, no weapons. Any coward can pick up a gun or a knife. It takes a man to stand alone with an empty hand."

The man sounded sincere. Ken gave him a curious look. "I almost believe you mean that."

"I do," Sagat replied. "It's the difference between me and that maniac Bison."

"If he's a maniac, why do you supply him with guns?" Ken asked.

"I like to keep my maniacs happy," Sagat replied with a smile.

The countdown began. Vega lowered his steel mask again. Apparently he wanted to keep his face pretty.

"So what's the story with this guy?" Ken asked.

"Vega?" Sagat said. "He was a matador in training, but he had a cruel streak."

"I would have thought you needed a cruel streak in his line of work," Ken said.

"Maybe, but not one like Vega's," Sagat said. "He had no discipline. He likes only one thing."

"Let me guess," Ken said. "Shopping?"

"Killing," Sagat replied coldly.

In the ring, Vega and Ryu began to circle each other. The bloodthirsty crowd began to roar. Weapons or no weapons, they wanted a fight to the death.

CRASH! There was a thunderous crash. Bodies started to hurl in all directions *outside* the ring. Ryu and Vega straightened up and watched in amazement as a huge, dark green tank smashed through a wall of the warehouse and stopped with its cannon right in Sagat's face.

The crowd stood in silent astonishment. Dust floated in the air, and pieces of wall debris slid from the tank's glistening armor.

The hatch popped up.

A light blue beret rose up, followed by Colonel Guile himself. Hands on hips, he gazed calmly at the warehouse full of criminals.

"You're all under arrest," he said.

In a flash, dozens of armed AN troopers flooded into the warehouse, quickly outnumbering the crowd.

Clank! Clatter! Plang! The sounds of weapons falling to the floor made a considerable racket as the hoodlums raised their hands over their heads. Ken leaned into Ryu.

"See?" he said in a low voice. "Didn't I tell you our luck would change?"

Five

The following day, Colonel Guile strode through the AN headquarters, dictating a letter to an aide who scurried behind him.

"*Monsieur et Madame Charlot. Le sacrifice de votre fils ne sera jamais oublié. Votre sacrifice sera avengé.* Sign and send it."

"Right away, sir." The aide nodded and turned back to her desk. Guile went through a doorway and stepped into a briefing room. His military staff was seated around a long table.

"Ten-shun!" an AN guard barked and the staff quickly rose to its feet.

"At ease," Guile said and took a seat at the head of the table. To his right, Cammy sat at a computer console, entering data. The pretty blonde lieutenant had been assisting the colonel since they'd met during Operation Desert Storm. Several years later she'd been abducted while on a secret intelligence mission in Bosnia. Guile had gone in and rescued her, but not before she'd been tortured and scarred for life.

Now, seeing the aide through the doorway, she leaned toward the commander.

"Colonel," she said, voicing what the rest of the staff was wondering, "are you really going to write to every mother of every soldier who died?"

"Yes," Guile replied. "But the letter I really want to write is to Bison's mother . . . only I don't think he had one."

The staff laughed. Guile glanced at a large clock winding down on the wall.

"The countdown clock?" he guessed.

"We want to keep it where we'll all see it," one of the staff members replied while a white-jacketed waiter filled glasses around the table with water.

Guile nodded. "New business?"

A young Japanese captain rose from his seat.

"Yes, Captain Sawada?" Guile said.

"Colonel, my commando team is at full readiness," Sawada reported. "But we need to know if the assault will be by land, sea, or air."

"I'm afraid that's the question of the day," Guile replied and turned toward his lieutenant. "What have you got for us, Cammy?"

The trim lieutenant rose and gestured toward a large video monitor in the corner showing aerial photography in various computer modes.

"Thanks to the colonel's, uh, unorthodox psychological warfare the other morning"—the words brought laughter from the staff—"we were able to get Bison to break radio silence. Unfortunately, not long enough to pinpoint the source of his signal. At this point all we can say for certain is that his base is hidden somewhere here, in the river delta region."

Using a pointer, Cammy gestured to a marshy region of land to the north.

"We'll have to go up there and search on the ground," Sawada said.

"No," Guile said. "That could take weeks. We have fewer than three days—"

"EEeeeee-yaaahhhhh!" Without warning, the waiter pulled a long knife and leaped onto the table, diving at Guile.

Crack! Crunch! Guile caught the attacker by the elbow and drove him face first into the table. The man twitched slightly and then lay motionless.

"Any other new business?" Guile asked. His staff stood with stunned expressions on their faces, staring at the body of the man lying on the table.

"All right, I have some," the colonel said. "How did this crud get in here?"

Guile looked hard at T. Hawk, who was usually in charge of security. The tall Native American stiffened.

"Sir! There is no excuse for this," he replied. "As officer in charge of security, I take full responsibility."

"Uh, excuse me." Cammy came forward. "If I may, Colonel, T. Hawk's not quite right. He was in the hospital for that head wound when the locals were hired. The Shadaloo liaison officer was supposed to vet the headquarters staff, but . . . obviously he didn't do it very well."

Guile turned to his security officer. "Is that right, Sergeant?"

"Well, yes, sir, but it's still no excuse," T. Hawk sputtered. "If I hadn't stuck my head up and caught that shrapnel—"

Guile smiled and gave him a mock slap in the face. He was lucky he had soldiers like this on his side who refused to make excuses and who even took responsibility for others' mistakes. Guile only hoped he would be a worthy commander for a team like this. Meanwhile,

Cammy moved to the man laying on the table and pulled open his shirt.

"Here's your explanation, sir," she said, gesturing at a large tattoo of a serpent curled around a dagger on the man's chest. "Shadaloo Tong."

"Viktor Sagat's organization," Guile said.

"Yes, sir."

"Refresh my memory, Lieutenant," Guile ordered.

"Before the civil war, Sagat was the absolute crime lord here," Cammy explained. "All criminal activities, including drugs, extortion, smuggling, and gambling, are controlled by the tong. But rather than stand up against Bison, Sagat decided to profit from him instead. Now he supplies Bison with all his weapons."

"Don't I have Sagat locked up in the stockade at this very moment?" Guile asked.

"Yes, sir," Cammy replied.

"And he's still pulling strings," Guile mused.

"Let me get him into an interrogation room," T. Hawk said with a growl. "I'll cut his strings for him."

"No, wait." Guile was getting an idea. "This could be the break we've been looking for. If Sagat runs guns to Bison, then he must know where Bison's secret command post is. All we have to do is infiltrate someone into his gang and follow the next shipment."

The staff members exchanged looks. Cammy cleared her throat.

"Excuse me, sir, but Sagat didn't get to the top of the Asian underworld by taking chances. Even in normal times he trusts no one. Now in the middle of this war he's bound to suspect anyone we try to plant on him. He's not exactly the type who makes new friends."

Guile had just begun to mull over this when sounds of

a commotion rose from the stockade outside.

"What's going on out there?" Guile asked T. Hawk, who stepped over to the window and looked down at the stockade outside the headquarters building. The stockade was basically a fortified courtyard for holding criminals until they could be processed. The ground was dirt, and a few old green tarps hanging overhead kept the rain out.

"Well, sir, unless I'm imagining things," the chief of security said, "I'd say we've got a full-scale riot in the stockade."

Guile rushed out of the room. He didn't need this now. They were wasting valuable time.

Six

A little while earlier, Ken and Ryu, dressed in blue prisoners' clothes, had moved through the stockade food line, pushing trays with their fellow detainees. On stone walls around them AN guards patrolled, keeping an eye on the prisoners below. Others stood on tall bamboo gun towers.

A cook slapped a large ladle of unidentifiable brown glop on their plates.

"I'm quoting you now," Ryu muttered to Ken. "You said, 'By this time tomorrow we'll be on a plane, sipping champagne and eating caviar and counting our money.'" He nodded down toward the end of the food line. "I guess the caviar must be down there."

"Yuck, yuck." Ken smirked.

"I just don't know why I listen to you," Ryu said.

"Because I have ideas," Ken replied.

"All your ideas ever do is get us close to being killed," Ryu said.

"And all you do is complain," Ken said, his voice filled with annoyance. "Yesterday you were worried you were gonna get stuck in the middle of a civil war. Presto, chango, today you're clean, well fed, and in protective custody. Now, what's wrong with that?"

Ryu saw something that gave him doubts. "It may be

custody, but I'm not so sure it's protective."

Ken followed his friend's eyes to a group of men. Sagat was in the middle of them, glaring at Ken and Ryu. Sagat whispered something to one of his men, who moved off and signaled someone. Ryu watched as the signal traveled from thug to thug. The future was starting to grow dim.

"I think I just lost my appetite," Ken muttered, putting down his tray.

He and Ryu started out of the food area, but a wall of grim-looking thugs forced them back in. Suddenly a canvas tarp fell from above, blocking off the food area from the MPs patrolling the stockade from above.

Ken and Ryu found themselves in deep shadow. The kitchen workers ducked beneath the counters.

"I guess lunch is over," Ken said. "Too bad, I was looking forward to seconds."

Thugs started to close in around them, the makeshift knives in their hands glinting faintly.

"How come *they* have weapons and we don't?" Ken whispered.

"Because they have friends around here," Ryu whispered back.

The thugs charged.

Whack! Whomp! Wham! Fighting back to back, Ken and Ryu kicked, smashed, chopped, and jabbed at the seemingly unending stream of thugs.

A burning sensation slashed through Ken's biceps as a thug cut him with a knife. Ken grabbed the man, snapped his arm behind his back, and threw him into three others.

Two men attacked Ryu, one from either side. He leaped in the air and did an aikido split, catching both in the Adam's apple. As he landed, he found Vega coming toward him with a crude jailhouse version of his claw strapped to his hand.

"Vega." Ryu went into a crouch. "I was afraid we'd never finish our fight."

"You *should* be afraid," Vega replied with a cold smile.

The claw whipped through the air. Ryu ducked. The claw scraped the brick wall, kicking up a shower of sparks. Ryu lunged up.

Whack! He caught Vega on the wrist and sent the claw flying. The handsome killer spun around, ready to take on Ryu barehanded. Ryu smiled. This *was* a fight he'd been waiting for.

"Back off! Back off!" Suddenly AN guards pushed their way through the crowd. Ryu felt hands grab him and pull him away from Vega. Well, there would always be tomorrow. . . .

Colonel Guile stood with T. Hawk and Cammy on a stairwell on the other side of the stockade yard. They'd just watched Ken and Ryu fight. Guile knew immediately that there was something different about those two.

"Who are they?" Guile asked.

T. Hawk opened a dossier. Inside were mug shots and confiscated passports. "Ken Masters and Ryu Hoshi. Couple of low-rent operators wanted for scams all around the Pacific rim. We took them in last night's sweep."

"Are they part of Sagat's organization?" Guile asked.

"Actually, no," T. Hawk replied. "They're both from pretty good backgrounds. Hoshi's from a big Japanese industrial family. He's college-educated. Masters' father is a politician back in the U.S."

"Black sheep?" Guile guessed.

"Couldn't speculate, sir."

"What were they doing with the Shadaloo Tong?" Guile asked.

"Got me," T. Hawk answered with a shrug. "But they sure weren't selling Girl Scout cookies."

Guile rubbed his chin. "What about that truckload of toy guns we confiscated? Could they have had something to do with that?"

"Could have," T. Hawk said.

Guile smiled. So these two men were scam artists, and nervy ones at that. They might have been scam artists, but chances were they came from backgrounds where good was valued over evil.

"Get 'em patched up and bring them to me," the colonel said. Then he turned to Cammy. "If Sagat won't trust any new friends . . . maybe he'll trust some new enemies."

Cammy frowned. She believed wholeheartedly in her boss. But sometimes she simply didn't understand him.

Dressed with a scarf on her head, sunglasses, and many strings of pearls, Chun-Li looked less like a news reporter and more like a wealthy tourist as she rode in a water taxi to the docks of Shadaloo City. The streets before her were crowded with people on foot, on bicycle, in rickshaws, and on motorbikes. In the daylight hours, business went on as normal.

Stepping off the taxi, she started to make her way down a crowded city street. Grimy workers and women lugging bundles stepped out of her way, and a line of ragtag street urchins followed behind her, offering to sell her trinkets and begging for money.

Chun-Li turned down an alley where a small truck was parked. Two large men hulked nearby. For a brief moment, Chun-Li felt a chill of fear, then she realized they were her crew, Balrog and Honda, in disguise.

"If it weren't for the fact that you're seven feet tall and about four hundred pounds, I might not have recognized you," she said to Honda.

"The one thing I can't do is make myself look like a midget," the technician replied.

"So, did we get it?" Chun-Li asked.

Honda nodded at Balrog, and together they pulled up a tarp at the back of the truck. Inside were several large wooden boxes marked DANGER—HI EXPLOSIVES.

Chun-Li grinned. "Looks like we got it."

The wound on Ken's arm was dressed. He and Ryu were cleaned up and issued new prison clothes. Now they stood on a dock behind the AN headquarters. Colonel Guile stood nearby as they watched a boatload of Shadaloo refugees pull in. Neither Ken nor Ryu knew why he was there.

"Uh, we waiting for someone?" Ken asked.

"I saw you two fight," Guile said. "I know you've been trained. What I don't know is whether it's all in your fists."

"We're pretty good with our feet, too," Ryu said, making a joke.

Guile didn't smile. He just pointed to his head. "Didn't your sensei put anything here?" He gestured to his heart. "Or here? Do you have any chi, or is it all smoke?"

Ryu glanced at Ken and didn't answer. What was this, kindergarten for martial arts?

43

"Look at them," Guile said. Ken and Ryu watched as the injured refugees were taken off the ship on stretchers. The walking wounded came next, hobbling on crutches or being pushed in wheelchairs. They were followed by dozens of emaciated-looking men and women with crying babies and children in tattered clothing.

"These are the minority who have survived Bison," Guile said. "No matter where they turn, there's a warlord, or a black marketeer, or worse. Now, maybe these people have a chance because they've made it to Shadaloo City. But those hostages Bison is holding don't even have that."

"What is this?" Ken asked. "A guilt trip?"

"Let's call it a reality check," Guile replied. He turned and started to follow the refugees into a large warehouse that had been outfitted as a field hospital. Doctors and nurses greeted the wounded and sick and tried to comfort them.

Ken and Ryu looked around and winced. Guile kept walking and tapped a finger on the dossiers he carried on both men. "Manila, Hong Kong, Shadaloo. You justify your little con games by telling yourselves that you've been stealing from criminals. But the criminals you rob have been preying on these people. Where does that put you on the food chain? Are you really the same as Sagat and Bison? Or am I right, and you're different?"

Ryu glanced back at the refugees. Men with parts of their arms or legs missing. Children with bloated, empty stomachs. He glanced at Ken, and they both winced. This was something they'd never thought about. Now both knew they'd never put it out of their minds.

"You're right, we're different," Ryu replied. "Can we leave now?"

Guile stopped and studied them. "The only way you two are leaving," he said with an odd smile, "is over my dead body."

Seven

The cold steel pneumatic doors opened, and Bison stepped into the laboratory of Dr. Dhalsim. Zangief followed a respectful distance behind. Chained, and shadowed by an armed guard, the former professor of genetics from the University of Calcutta stood at a computer console. Beyond the console was a large white brainwashing chamber with round, greenish glass portholes. Through those portholes one could see Carlos Blanka, his head covered with virtual reality goggles and earphones. Long plastic IV tubes snaked down into his arms.

"So, Dr. Dhalsim, how is your research today?" Bison asked.

"The same," the scientist muttered. "Corrupted, warped . . . my science twisted to serve perversion instead of peace."

The conversation made Zangief's brow crease. The man was a physical giant, but mentally, completely naive. Meanwhile, General Bison pouted at Dr. Dhalsim's hard words.

"Doctor, how can you say that?" he asked.

"Very easily," Dhalsim replied. "Sometimes I wonder if you know the irony behind all this. That when your men kidnapped me in Stockholm I was there to warn the

46

Nobel committee against just the sort of deviant work you now force me to do."

Bison stepped closer and put his hand on the doctor's shoulder. "I see that you are not happy. Tell you what. After I crush my enemies, we'll see about getting you published. That should cheer you up."

"Hardly," Dr. Dhalsim muttered.

"Now let us have a look at our patient," Bison said. The mad warlord peered over the console and into the chamber where Charlie Blanka sat, strapped to a cushioned chair. Bison glanced back down at the computer and medical readouts.

"His brain functions are very low," he observed.

"Perhaps if your soldiers hadn't beaten him senseless they'd be a bit higher," Dhalsim replied.

"You are a pessimist," Bison replied with a shake of his head. "You look at this and see a brain that is half empty. I am an optimist. I see a brain that is half full. And once you fill it completely, our Captain Carlos Blanka will be a perfect soldier."

"You mean a perfect killer," Dhalsim corrected him.

"Let's not quibble over words," Bison said with a shrug.

In the brainwashing chamber, Blanka whimpered and shifted against the restraints.

"Was that a reaction to the programming?" Bison asked. "What is he receiving?"

"See for yourself." The doctor hit some keys on the console, and rapid-fire images began to splash across the monitors.

Bison was entranced as a montage of mankind's worst violence from antiquity forward passed before his eyes. The Roman Colosseum, massacres, pogroms, concentra-

47

tion camps, human slaughters, Russia, Germany, Bosnia, Somalia, followed by a portrait gallery of history's worst villains — Attila the Hun, Nero, Hitler, Stalin, and finally . . . Bison himself!

The warlord turned away from the monitor, perplexed. "This is merely educational software. Why does our guinea pig find it disturbing?"

"Because, unlike you, he's not psychotic."

Whap! The backhand slap caught Dhalsim on the jaw and knocked him onto the floor. The warlord stood over him, glowering.

"You take too many risks, Doctor," Bison said with a growl. "Do not presume so much on my good nature. Now that Blanka's brain is in the process of becoming a killing machine, my loyal scientists will start on his body."

As Bison said this, several younger scientists in white Bison lab uniforms entered the brainwashing chamber and began to disconnect the IV lines running into Blanka's arms.

"What are they doing?" Dhalsim asked with a gasp while rising to his feet. "He needs those nutrients. Without them he'll . . ."

The doctor's words trailed off as he watched the scientists attach new IV lines from thick bags labeled DANGER—DNA MUTAGENS—USE EXTREME CAUTION and ANABOLIC PLASMA—WARNING—TOXIC AT HIGH DOSES.

"Without them he'll do very nicely," Bison finished Dhalsim's sentence. "Don't worry, Doctor, our baby is going to grow up big and strong . . . *very strong.*"

Bison turned to his scientists. "How long will it take until his muscle mass has doubled?"

"Twenty-four hours, sir," one of the scientists replied.

"Very good," said the warlord. "In twenty-four hours he is going to be field-tested. In combat."

The scientists nodded eagerly. Unlike Dr. Dhalsim, they did not work for the warlord against their wills. In fact, they were loyal, dedicated, and just about as demented as Bison himself. The warlord spun on his heels and headed out. Dr. Dhalsim gazed at the poor man in the brainwashing chamber. The terrible greenish DNA mutagens and pink anabolic plasma flowed into his veins, transforming him into precisely the kind of protoplasmic aberration Dhalsim had been haunted by for years. And yet here he was, aiding and abetting the cause. The doctor felt his shoulders sag with self-disgust at what he'd become.

Zing! A painful bolt of electricity in his side caused him to jump.

"Back to work," muttered the guard who watched over him.

Dhalsim nodded, and the guard slid his electric prod back into its holster.

Out in the hallway, Zangief's confusion finally poured out as he followed his great leader. Zangief had joined the Soviet Army at age fourteen, so his entire life had been filled with propaganda and lies. Now, he believed in Bison, his leader and savior.

"Dhalsim was disrespectful, General. He called you evil names. Why do you permit this?"

"You must sympathize with Dhalsim," Bison replied in an avuncular mood. "You see, he actually believes the poisonous lies about me that have been spread by my enemies. He doesn't understand that I am the only one who can save the world from the Allied Nations tyranny."

In his own, semi-intelligent way, Zangief was touched by this. "The poor man. Someday he know truth like me."

"We can only pray," Bison said with a roll of his eyes.

The members of the tong, chained together in small groups, were led out of the stockade. Sagat and Vega led the way. Several groups back, Ken and Ryu followed. They were all led toward a waiting truck. Behind the truck's cab was a large wire cage used for transporting criminals.

"Take them to the harbor," Guile ordered the truck's driver. "The navy has a brig waiting for them."

The commander waved at the tong leader. "*Bon voyage*, Sagat. Enjoy the sea air."

"This isn't over, Guile," Sagat snarled back. "I own this city."

"Well, I'm the repo man," Guile replied with a smile. "And I just took it back. Looks like you're out of business."

The commander went back into the headquarters. Ryu gave Ken a sour look.

"You just *had* to come to this country, didn't you?" he said angrily.

"Man, don't you *ever* stop complaining?" Ken asked. "I really don't understand you."

"The only thing I don't understand," Ryu said, "is why I listen to you. You can't think, and you can't fight."

"Oh, yeah?" Ken spat back. "Well, I'll tell you what I think. I think I'm sick of your mouth!"

Despite the chains, the two men began to struggle. T. Hawk and an MP jumped into the fray and separated them.

"Knock it off, dirtbags!" T. Hawk shouted. "Get in the truck."

Ken and Ryu climbed into the cage behind the truck. In the shadows inside, their animosity quickly disappeared as Ryu held up a small key ring. Sitting across from them, Sagat's eyes went wide.

"How?" he gasped.

"Hey, I was a pretty good pickpocket as a kid," Ryu said as he started to unlock the chains around Ken's feet, and then his own.

"Throw me the key," Sagat said, hissing.

"Get real," Ryu muttered, sliding the keys into his pocket.

"I'm serious," Sagat insisted. "I'll make it worth your while."

"Oh, yeah, *that's* a good one." Ken nodded dubiously. "And I'll bet you'll want us to come to your warehouse to collect it, like last time."

"No, no." Sagat shook his head vehemently. "Forget our past! I can help you escape the city! You need me!"

"Ha!" Ken laughed. "You think I can't find my way out of this place on my own?"

"Can you?" Ryu asked.

Ken and Ryu shared a questioning look.

"Hey," Ken said, "when have I ever let you down?"

"When haven't you?" Ryu asked back.

Some of Sagat's men smiled.

"You'll never make it out of the country without my help," Sagat said.

"Oh, yeah?" Ken said, puffing up his chest.

Ryu tapped him on the shoulder. "Did it ever occur to you that the great Colonel Guile still has our passports?"

"Oh, right." Ken's chest sagged.

"Passports?" Sagat smiled. "A simple matter. I could have new ones for you in a matter of hours."

Ken nodded and glanced at his partner. "That *would* make it a lot easier."

"Okay, Sagat, here you go." Ryu passed the keys to the tong's leader. "But we want those passports."

"We're taking you at your word, Sagat," Ken said. "Which is probably the dumbest thing we've done since we tried to sell you toy guns."

"You won't be sorry," Sagat replied, hastily unlocking his shackles and those of his men.

A moment later Ryu and Vega jumped off the back of the truck.

Chong! Vega took down an AN guard with a vicious kick to the head while Ryu yanked the truck driver out of his seat and jumped in the cab. He jammed the truck in gear and started to drive through the compound, heading toward the gates.

"No, you don't!" T. Hawk jumped onto the running board and tried to grab the steering wheel. As they grappled with each other, the truck veered forward. Ryu grabbed T. Hawk's pistol from the sergeant's belt. MPs took aim, but another yelled to hold their fire for fear of hitting Sergeant Hawk.

CRASH! The truck smashed through some sawhorses and careened around the corner in front of the AN headquarters. The collision knocked T. Hawk off the truck.

"Hey, Ryu!" Ken shouted from the back of the truck.

Ryu looked in the sideview mirror and saw his friend hanging out the back of the cage, waving.

"Throw me the gun!" Ken yelled.

Ryu tossed T. Hawk's pistol out the window, and Ken caught the weapon.

The compound gates loomed ahead. As Ryu steered the truck toward them, Colonel Guile ran out into the street and drew a bead on the oncoming truck. AN soldiers aimed their rifles.

"Don't shoot!" T. Hawk yelled to them. "You'll hit the Colonel!"

The commotion brought Chun-Li running from inside the media center. She couldn't believe what she was seeing! With only a pistol cupped in his hand, Colonel Guile was trying to face down the truck speeding straight toward him!

Blam! Blam! Guile fired.

Hanging out of the back of the truck, Ken drew T. Hawk's pistol and aimed.

Blam! Blam! The shots struck Colonel Guile directly in the chest, spinning him away from the truck.

Chun-Li gasped. She had seen enough violence in her life to know a dead man when she saw one, and Colonel Guile was definitely a dead man. Stunned, she still had the presence of mind to yank a wireless mike from her blouse. As the truck barreled past, she rolled forward like an acrobat beside it and smacked the mike against a wheelwell.

The mike held, and Chun-Li rolled to the side, just barely escaping the truck's tires. Balrog and Honda rushed toward her, but she was already rising to her feet and running to the body of the man who had promised to bring them all peace.

Eight

"Bisonopolis," the warlord announced with a satisfied smile. Before him on a table was a model of the future, of his future. The abandoned temple stood at its center, but it was now surrounded by high-rise buildings, sculpted landscaping, tennis courts, and golf courses.

"And Bisonland?" the warlord asked, turning toward his architect, a young bearded German lad wearing wire rim glasses and the uniform of Bison's staff.

"From the monorail here," the young man said, pointing at the monorail station, "it will make three stops at your theme park: The Hall of Villains, Tragic Mountain, and Deathcot Center."

"Excellent," Bison said, circling the model with a metal pointer. "The temple above us was a wonder of the ancient world. Bisonopolis will be the wonder of *my* world."

The warlord stopped and scowled.

"Is something wrong, sir?" the architect asked.

"The Galleria Bison," the warlord muttered.

"The mall?" The architect frowned. "I thought you were pleased with it."

"The food court should be larger," Bison said. "All the big franchises will want in."

Through the open door to the fortress control room came dramatic news-breaking music accompanied by a television voice: *"We interrupt our regular broadcast with a special bulletin from Shadaloo City . . ."*

Bison looked up, interested. Through the doorway he could see his favorite news reporter appear on the bank of monitors. Normally the picture of collected coolness, the pretty young Chun-Li Zang actually looked rattled.

"Dateline, Shadaloo City, Shadaloo, Southeast Asia," she began. *"The world is in shock at the news that Colonel William F. Guile has been killed. . . . "*

Startled by the unexpected development, Bison dropped the pointer. He stepped to the doorway to get a better look.

"It happened just thirty minutes ago," Chun-Li went on, *"during a jailbreak by Viktor Sagat, the crime lord who has been the principal arms supplier for renegade General M. Bison. It was hoped that the Allied Nations forces would restore order here and that Colonel Guile would be able to free the sixty-three hostages now held by Bison in a countdown to death. But after today's shocking tragedy, nothing is certain . . . except that Bison's mad threats will continue . . . and that the new AN commander's first order of business will be to bury Colonel Guile. For GNT, this is Chun-Li Zang."*

How touching, Bison thought with a sigh. He raised his remote and lowered the audio on the video screens. Then he stood in silence, digesting the news.

"That's great news, General!" Dee Jay cried. "Congratulations!"

Bison nodded slowly, knowing the Jamaican electronics tech was only trying to score Brownie points.

"On the contrary," Bison replied. "I mourn. I was hoping to face Guile personally on the battlefield. One

gentleman warrior to another in respectful combat."
Bison clenched his fists. "Then I would snap his spine."

The warlord shook his head sadly. "Ah, the road not taken." He snapped his fingers. "Bring me my field armor."

Several pretty acolytes immediately stepped forward and started to snap the armor on Bison's shoulders, arms, and legs. Bison seemed to be in a pensive, reflective mood.

"Why?" he asked no one in particular. "Why do they still call me a 'warlord'? And why 'mad'? All I want to do is create the perfect genetic soldier. Not for power, not for evil, but for *good!*"

The guards around him nodded obediently.

"Carlos Blanka will be the first of many," Bison stated, his voice rising. "They will march out of my laboratory and under my leadership sweep away every adversary, every creed and nation, until the entire planet is in the loving grip of the Pax Bisonica!"

The guards glanced furtively at each other, but Bison caught their looks. They were soldiers, not intellectuals. They couldn't be expected to know that in Latin Pax Bisonica would mean the period of peace the world would soon embrace under the benign rule of Bison.

"Peace will reign," Bison said, his voice growing softer. "War will end forever. All humanity will bow to me in humble gratitude."

A guard came forward and whispered something in Dee Jay's ear. The electronics whiz turned to his leader. "Excuse me, General, the convoy is ready to escort you to The Thieves' Market."

The warlord raised his remote to the screen and flicked the image to Dr. Dhalsim's laboratory. The doctor appeared with his back to the camera as he worked at his computer. In the background, Carlos Blanka remained in the brainwashing chamber. He appeared to be larger than before.

"Doctor," Bison said, "I will be gone until dawn. I want the subject ready for testing the moment I return."

With his back to the camera, Dhalsim nodded. Bison felt a tug of annoyance at the man's insolence.

"Dhalsim!" he barked.

The scientist turned and faced the camera with a startled expression.

"That's better," said the warlord. "You will look at me when I address you."

Dr. Dhalsim's eyes narrowed with anger. "You've murdered this boy once already. If you put him into combat before I run diagnostics, you'll kill him again."

"Don't worry, Doctor," Bison assured him, "I'm going to start him out with something easy."

"Like what?" Dr. Dhalsim asked.

"Like"—a demented smile grew on Bison's face—"killing the hostages."

Dhalsim's jaw dropped and his skin turned pale. If Bison used Blanka to kill the hostages, then, for all intents and purposes, Dhalsim was killing them as well.

The sun was going down. Outside the AN headquarters in Shadaloo City, news crews and reporters milled around restlessly, waiting for some word on the Allied Nations' plans now that Colonel Guile was dead.

The GNT news feed to the mobile van was coming in broken up, so Chun-Li had climbed up through the roof hatch and was checking the antenna wires for a loose connection.

"How's it going up there?" Honda called from inside.

"I think I've found the problem," Chun-Li called back. "How does it look down there?"

"Can't tell yet," Honda yelled back.

Rap! Rap! Someone banged on the side of the van, and Chun-Li looked over the side to find Sergeant T. Hawk looking up at her.

"Five minutes to curfew, ma'am," the sergeant informed her. "If you're not out of here by then, I'm impounding this vehicle and you along with it."

"I'm very sorry, Sergeant," Chun-Li replied. "We just couldn't get a clear fix on the satellite. We'll be out before curfew. I promise."

Knowing that a little female charm never hurt, Chun-Li gave him a warm smile and batted her eyelashes.

T. Hawk smiled back . . . and set his stopwatch. "That's five minutes. Starting *now!*"

The smile vanished from Chun-Li's face. These AN troops were simply *too* well trained. Meanwhile, T. Hawk turned to the rest of the crowd.

"Listen up, people!" he shouted. Once again he started to give them the curfew warning.

"Hey, Li," Balrog called from inside the van. "I think you got it."

"I'm coming down to take a look," Chun-Li said. She descended back into the van. Honda and Balrog were jammed inside, huddled around a scanning screen. They were packed in there like sardines.

Very, very *large* sardines.

"I hope we're making progress," Chun-Li said, pulling the hatch closed above her. "We just got the official five-minute warning."

"Relax," Honda muttered, "they don't got a jail in this

town that can hold me."

"Not unless they keep him supplied with unlimited hoagies," Balrog added, giving the bigger man a playful nudge.

"Hey, watch the elbow," Honda grumbled.

"What do you want me to do? Cut it off?" Balrog shot back. "There's no place else to put it."

"Enough, you two," Chun-Li said, pointing at the scanner. "How about getting this thing to work?"

Honda flicked a switch. "Ta-da!"

The screen flickered to life, and a map of Shadaloo Province appeared on the screen. A small glowing red dot moved slowly across it.

"You're a genius!" Chun-Li gave Honda an affectionate rub on the head. "There's our wireless mike."

"Looks like the truck's on the coast highway heading north," Balrog said.

"Any good guesses as to where they're headed?" Chun-Li asked.

Honda and Balrog looked at each other and were struck simultaneously with the answer. "The Thieves' Market!"

Chun-Li nodded. "Yes, that has to be it."

Suddenly the picture broke up with rising bands of static.

"Darn!" Chun-Li leaned forward and tapped the screen with her knuckle. "There's that interference again! Guess it's time to go back on the roof."

"Wait." Balrog peered closely at it. "Correction. That's not interference. It's too steady."

Now Chun-Li gave it a closer look. The cameraman was right. Whatever was breaking up their signal was too constant to be random.

"So what's causing it?" Honda asked.

The answer struck Chun-Li like a bolt. "Unless all of our equipment needs a tune-up, we're not the only ones who put a tracking device on that truck."

"Huh?" Honda frowned.

"She's right," Balrog said. "We've got two signals mixing up. That's what's causing the distortion."

"Wait a minute," Honda said. "I thought I was the electronics tech here."

"Let's analyze the other signal," Chun-Li said.

Balrog's fingers flew over the keyboard like a concert pianist.

"Show-off," Honda muttered.

"You could do it, too," Balrog replied, "if you didn't have fingers the size of bananas."

"Chill, dude," Honda said, holding up his massive hands, "before these 'bananas' close around your neck."

"Hey, we're all on the same side here," Chun-Li reminded them.

"Yeah, the heavy side," Balrog said, peering at an oscilloscope. "Okay, here's the analysis. Steady flux, narrow bandwidth. Looks like it's aimed at—"

Balrog frowned.

"Aimed at what?" Chun-Li asked.

"This doesn't make sense," Balrog said.

"Leave that up to me," Chun-Li said.

"Well, unless I'm totally off, it's aimed right back here," Balrog said. "At AN headquarters."

"Here?" Honda frowned. "That makes no sense at all."

On the contrary, it was clear to Chun-Li that it did make sense to someone. They just had to find out who.

Rap! Rap!

Someone was knocking on the driver's side window.

Chun-Li didn't have to look to know who it was.

"It's Sergeant T. Hawk," Balrog said. "Time to bail."

Chun-Li pushed Honda toward the driver's seat. "You drive."

"Hey, I was gonna eat," Honda complained.

"Later," Chun-Li said, giving Balrog a nudge. "You're in the passenger seat."

"What is this?" Balrog asked.

"Just go," said Chun-Li.

Honda got behind the wheel and started to drive. In the back of the van, Chun-Li kept her eyes on the scanner while she started to unbutton her blouse. She glanced up and noticed that Honda was watching in the rearview mirror.

"Watch the road!" Chun-Li ordered.

Honda grinned but looked away.

"I don't know what you find so interesting," Chun-Li muttered as she changed her clothes. "You've only seen me do this about a hundred times."

"Hey, there are some things I never lose my appetite for," Honda quipped.

"Like hoagies," Balrog said.

"Well, you should have other things on your mind right now," Chun-Li chastised him, only half seriously. "That second homing signal bothers me. Personally, I don't like mysteries. There's always a murder before the last chapter."

"What do you want us to do?" Balrog asked.

"You two follow our signal," Chun-Li said as she adjusted the skintight black ninja outfit she'd just pulled on. "I'm sure it will lead you to The Thieves' Market."

"And we just walk in and say, 'Hi'?" Balrog asked.

"You can do better than that," Chun-Li said.

"Infiltrate."

"Why do I think they might notice a seven-foot, four-hundred-pound sumo trying to infiltrate?" Honda asked.

"All right," Chun-Li said, "if you can't infiltrate, then entertain."

"Entertain?" Balrog scowled. "Darn, I left my harpsichord at home."

"Be resourceful," Chun-Li said. "I know you'll think of something. I'll catch up with you at The Thieves' Market."

"Catch up?" Balrog raised a curious eyebrow.

"Yes. Right now I'm going to find out who's playing games with us." Chun-Li reached for the roof hatch and pushed it open. She started to climb up.

"Watch your back, Li," Honda said, glancing at her in the rearview.

Chun-Li paused for a second. "I didn't know you cared."

"We don't," Balrog said with a wink. "But you're the only one who can sign our expense accounts."

Chun-Li grinned and climbed onto the roof of the moving van. It was dark now, and in her black ninja suit she was barely visible. The van stopped at the gate leaving the AN compound. A guard raised the traffic arm to let the van into traffic. At that moment Chun-Li leaped silently off the roof and onto the archway above the gate. Crouching low, without making a sound, she crept along the wall toward the headquarters building.

Somewhere in there was the answer. She just had to make sure she didn't get killed trying to find it.

Nine

Chun-li followed the top of the wall until she found an open second-floor window. She slipped through it and into a dimly lit corridor. Now what? From a pocket she drew out a device about the size of a small calculator. It was a miniature scanner, like the one they used in the van. The homing signal came in strong. It seemed to originate from somewhere in the basement of the building.

Chun-Li found a stairway and started down it, her feet padding more quietly than a cat's. A door banged somewhere below. The sound of rapid footsteps coming up the steps toward her caused her to duck behind a doorway. That blond lieutenant, Cammy, dashed past, coming so close to Chun-Li that she practically grazed her outfit. Chun-Li slipped back into the stairwell. Outside, in the halls, AN headquarters was filled with people. Most of them, hopefully, would be using the elevator.

The miniscanner led her to a silver door in the basement marked MORGUE. Chun-Li frowned. This made no sense at all.

Chun-Li closed her hand over the cold silver doorknob and turned. The lock clicked and the door opened. She slipped in and let the door close.

The room was dark and cold, illuminated only by

scant rays of moonlight through a window. Chun-Li pressed her back against the wall and waited for her eyes to adjust to the dark. Despite all her training, her heart was beating fast and her breaths were short and cloudy in the chilly air. A thin sheen of perspiration broke out across her forehead. The truth was, she *hated* dark, cold rooms filled with bodies.

As her eyes adjusted, she could see the metal cabinets along the wall, each drawer precisely the size necessary for the storage of a body. Rows of industrial shelves held large jars containing various body parts. Not far from the wall was a table with a body covered with a sheet.

Chun-Li caught her breath. Oh, no! It *had* to be Guile! She fought back the desire to bolt out the door and instead looked down at the scanner. The signal was stronger than ever and seemed to be coming from across the room.

She took a deep breath and let it out slowly. For the sake of all those who had died like Colonel Guile, and for the sake of all those whose lives were in danger . . . she had to get control of herself and press forward.

Eyes locked on the miniscanner, she stepped tentatively across the room, trying not to look at anything else. Her concentration was so focused that she didn't even notice how close she came to the body lying on the table.

There! On a stand next to the table was a small receiver. This *had* to be the one tracking the second signal. So someone in AN headquarters was tracking the truck after all.

But who?

The answer came in a most unusual way. . . .

A hand shot up from the body and grabbed her arm!

"Ahhhhhhhhh!" A scream ripped from Chun-Li's

throat.

Colonel Guile sat up, barechested in the dark, letting the sheet slide away. "If I wouldn't give you an interview when I was alive," he said with a chuckle, "what made you think I'd give you one when I was dead?"

Angered by the scare he'd given her, Chun-Li yanked her arm out of his grip and glared at him.

"You scared me!" she gasped, still trembling.

"Hey, come on, I couldn't resist," Guile said with a smile and a wink.

Chun-Li felt her anger fade. He certainly could be charming when he made the effort. And now the events of that afternoon were beginning to make sense.

"Of course," she said with a knowing nod. "Those two young men . . . they were the only ones who were not in the tong. One of them 'killed' you. They're working for you, aren't they?"

Guile slid off the table and stood before her, eyeing the black ninja outfit. "Are you asking me as a reporter? Or as something else?"

Chun-Li had no intention of answering. Just at that moment, the morgue door swung open and Sergeant T. Hawk dashed in, drawn by Chun-Li's scream.

"You?" He frowned at the sight of Chun-Li in black.

"Ms. Zang has a nice fashion sense, don't you think?" Guile asked his aide.

"Not bad," T. Hawk replied, clearly appreciating the way the outfit hugged her body.

"If you gentlemen are finished discussing my wardrobe," Chun-Li said with a scowl, "I'll be on my way."

She turned to go, but T. Hawk immediately stepped in her way.

"What is this?" Chun-Li asked, although she had a pretty good feeling for what was going on.

"Sergeant," Guile said, "take the mysterious Ms. Zang into custody. She's to be held in complete isolation until further notice."

Chun-Li spun around, her eyes wide. "No, wait, please, Colonel, don't."

"I'm sorry, Ms. Zang," Guile replied. "But I don't know what you're doing here in that outfit or what your motives are. Obviously you're now privy to information that can endanger my operation and the lives of the men undertaking it. I can't just let you walk out of here."

"All right, then I'll tell you what you want to know," Chun-Li said. "You're right. I'm not here to cover the news. I don't want a story about Bison."

Guile looked surprised. "Then what *do* you want?"

"I want his head."

Guile crossed his arms and nodded slowly. The explanation didn't surprise him in the least. A madman like Bison couldn't destroy lives forever without engendering some sort of vigilante revenge.

"It's taken me twenty years to get this far," Chun-Li continued. "You can't lock me up now, not when I'm this close."

Her yearning and pain were so real that Guile could almost reach out and touch them. But at this point his operation had a far better shot at cutting Bison down than one young woman dressed in a ninja outfit.

"Take her away," Guile said.

"Yes, sir." T. Hawk took her firmly by the arm and started to lead her toward the door. It opened as Cammy hurried in, pistol drawn. She, too, had heard Chun-Li's scream.

"Cammy, go with T. Hawk and Ms. Zang," Guile ordered. "We don't need any more problems."

"Yes, sir." Cammy took Chun-Li's other arm.

As they went out the door, Chun-Li turned back toward Guile. "I should have known you wouldn't understand," she said angrily.

"I understand better than you know," Guile replied. "But this war isn't about your personal vendetta."

T. Hawk and Cammy led her out. Guile turned to pull his shirt on. No, it wasn't about Chun-Li's personal vendetta. It was about *his*. He was going to save his friend Charlie Blanka if it was the last thing he did.

"Hey!" It was T. Hawk, shouting from the hall. Something must have gone wrong.

Guile rushed to the morgue door. Swinging it open, he saw a figure in black doing a series of rapid backflips down the outside corridor.

Crash! One last backflip and Chun-Li sailed through a window at the end of the hall and disappeared into the dark.

Humiliated that she'd gotten away, T. Hawk hung his head. But Guile could only smile. So there really *was* a ninja inside that suit.

"Sorry, sir," T. Hawk muttered. "What a screwup."

"No." Guile grinned despite himself. "What a *woman*."

On a remote piece of land up the coast, where access could be gained only via one heavily guarded road, stood The Thieves' Market. Here, among makeshift tents and shacks, unsavory merchants sold everything from guns and plastic explosives to prisoners and stolen computer access codes. Here, the well-heeled buyer with a taste for mayhem could pick up a few red-tipped cruise missiles, a heavily armed helicopter, or even a little Russian plutonium to set at the heart of a homemade nuclear device.

At the center of the camp stood the largest and newest tent, flying the silver and red banner of General M. Bison. Parked next to it were several trucks loaded with fresh munitions, recently delivered by Viktor Sagat.

The tent was lit by candles and small fires. Music was supplied by a small band of musicians playing drums, cymbals, and flutes. In the middle of the tent, on a dais, Bison, in his armor, sat on a raised throne while a mixed and motley bag of thieves, guests, and guards milled about. Near him, seated on a less ornate and lower chair, was Sagat. Bison insisted that he attend the party as a way of thanking him for the newest shipment of deadly supplies.

Across from them, on a small raised stage of black and white tiles, the "Benbelli Brothers" performed magic tricks that mostly involved throwing their lovely female assistant around in the air and randomly smashing large pieces of furniture to bits. The Benbellis were both large men dressed in turbans and robes. Their curvaceous assistant wore a tight purple outfit with a mask made of pink feathers.

Not far away, Ken and Ryu sat, watching the show.

"Don't they look familiar?" Ryu asked.

"Who?" Ken replied, munching on a drumstick.

"The Benbellis and their cute assistant," Ryu said.

Ken glanced up at the stage. "Maybe we saw them in Singapore or somewhere."

"No, it was more recent," Ryu said.

"Well, I don't know," Ken said. "I think I would have remembered the babe. She's hot stuff."

Ryu noticed that the fighter Vega, seated near Sagat,

was giving them a disgusted look.

"What happened, Vega?" Ryu asked. "Eat something that disagreed with you?"

"What are you doing here?" Vega asked.

"Hey, if it wasn't for us, you'd be in the brig right now," Ken said.

"I don't trust either of you." Vega spat. "And *you* owe me a fight."

"It's a rain check," Ryu replied.

On the stage, the Benbelli Brothers said something about preparing for their greatest illusion. Accompanied by their masked assistant, they bounded off the stage and disappeared, to be replaced by half a dozen scantily clad dancing girls. Ken looked around, meeting unfriendly glares from every direction.

Turning to Ryu, he spoke in a low voice: "This place makes downtown Detroit look like Disneyland."

"Be cool, man," Ryu whispered back.

"Oh, sure," Ken said. "Meanwhile, the only thing I can't figure out is whose lowlifes are gonna kill us first, Sagat's or Bison's."

Before Ryu could answer, he heard an angry grumble behind him. Turning around, he found Zangief gnawing on the leg of a boar.

"Did you say General Bison was lowlife?" the huge man grunted as he wiped his mouth with the back of his hand.

"*Low*life?" Ken swallowed. "No, no, I said *great* life. What a great life it is working for General Bison."

"You have served with General Bison?" Zangief looked surprised. "Why Zangief not know you?"

Ken glanced nervously at Ryu.

"Uh, you don't remember that night in Shadaloo

69

City?" Ryu asked. Several thugs turned to listen, and now he addressed all of them. "Zangief here wasn't satisfied with the two women he'd already met. He had to steal ours, too."

The thugs nodded, impressed.

Zangief counted on his fingers. "Zangief meet . . . er, four women?"

"Believe it." Ken nodded.

Zangief grinned and spread his huge arms, pulling them into a bear hug. "Little buddies!"

Ugh! Ah! Crash! Near them a fight broke out among some of the more feisty guests. Bison's armed guards were on them in an instant, cracking their skulls with the butts of their rifles and dragging them away.

Ken poked Ryu gently in the ribs. "I think it's time we got out of here."

"Guile was right," Ryu replied, giving his friend a critical look. "You have forgotten everything our sensei taught us about trust and honor."

"Our sensei also talked about the 'dragon punch' where a fighter's inner spirit gets released," Ken reminded him.

"Yes, the sho-ryu-ken. So?"

"So I think dragons and honor have a lot in common. They're both imaginary."

"Look, we made a deal with Guile," Ryu said. "We're in this thing until we get the homing device into Bison's fortress. As soon as we've done that, and Guile can find the place, we get our passports back and we're free to go, okay?"

His pal didn't answer. Ryu turned and discovered Ken wasn't even there. His friend was pushing through the crowd toward a corner of the tent. Now Ryu saw why—

70

the Benbelli Brothers' pretty assistant was beckoning Ken toward her. Ryu swore to himself and got up to follow. It seemed as if all he ever did anymore was keep his buddy out of trouble.

Ryu moved through the crowd. Ahead, he saw Ken follow the girl through the folds of the tent. Had it been any other occasion, he would have backed off and minded his own business.

But not tonight. Not with all these bad guys around.

Ryu reached the fold in the tent and found the opening. He pushed his way through. A dozen yards away was a smaller tent belonging to those Benbelli clowns. Ryu caught a glimpse of Ken going in.

Sorry to spoil your fun, buddy, Ryu thought as he swept back the canvas cover of the Benbellis' tent.

Whomp! Something huge hit and threw him to the ground. The next thing Ryu knew he was pinned to the earth by the strongest man he'd ever encountered.

Ten

Despite the overwhelming odds against him, Ryu started to struggle. Next, he felt the sharp edge of a knife against his throat.

"Stop fighting or die," a female voice ordered.

"I hate multiple choices," Ryu said. The massive hands holding him down let up while someone yanked Ryu's arms behind him and tied his hands with rope. Ryu looked up. The pretty acrobat he had been admiring earlier was holding the knife on him. A few feet away, Ken lay on the ground with his hands tied by the "Benbelli brothers."

"We don't want to hurt you," Chun-Li addressed them both.

"Well, you sure have a funny way of showing that," Ryu said.

Chun-Li ignored him. "We know you're working for Colonel Guile."

Ryu blinked with shock. No one was supposed to know that. And why did she look so familiar?

Chun-Li leaned closer. "You may not believe me, but we're your friends."

"My friends don't tie me up," Ken shot back, then remembered something. "Well, there *was* this girl in Miami once—"

"It was Atlanta, birdbrain," Ryu corrected him.

"No, man, I'm sure it was Miami," Ken said.

"Shut up!" Chun-Li snapped.

"But you should have seen her," Ken said.

"I don't want to know about it," Chun-Li replied impatiently.

Ryu kept staring at her. He was *sure* he knew her from somewhere. Then it hit him. "Wait a minute," he said. "I know you. You're that newscaster on Global News Television, Chun-Li." He twisted around and looked at the men who'd just tied his hands. "And you . . . you're Edmund Honda, the sumo from Hawaii. You almost made Yokozuna."

"Until the Shadaloo Tong destroyed my reputation," Honda said bitterly.

"How?" Ryu asked.

"They had a betting scam going," Honda said. "They told me I had to tank a match. I wouldn't do it, so they made sure I'd never wrestle again."

"They did the same thing to me," said Balrog. "Ruined my boxing career."

Ken looked up at Chun-Li. "Let me guess. They ruined your figure skating career?"

"Don't try to be cute," Chun-Li snapped at him.

"That's like telling Stimpy not to cough up hairballs," Ryu cracked.

"All right, enough!" Chun-Li shouted impatiently. "All you need to know is that the weapons and munitions Bison and Sagat deal in have brought misery to thousands. And in ten minutes those same weapons are going to send them straight to hell. You've had your warning."

"Time to prepare the truck," Honda said.

Honda and Balrog started out of the tent.

Chun-Li stood with her hands on her hips and stared at Ryu and Ken as if not sure what to do with them.

"Uh, just out of curiosity," Ken said, "you know that Sagat and Bison are in the next tent with several hundred armed men. Just how are you three going to send them straight to hell?"

"*We* won't. But their shipment of weapons will, with a very big bang." Chun-Li smiled.

"Oh, I think I get it," Ken said.

"If you don't, you will soon," Chun-Li said. Then she reached behind Ken and Ryu with the knife and quickly cut the ropes binding their hands. Ryu and Ken got up and looked at her in astonishment.

"You mean we can go?" Ken asked, mystified.

"Quickly, if I were you," Chun-Li warned him.

"Well, okay, but I'd still like to get your phone number," Ken said.

"Go!" Chun-Li shouted at him.

"Come on." Ryu grabbed his buddy by the collar and yanked him out of the tent.

Ken went with a shrug. "Guess I'm not her type."

"Consider yourself lucky," Ryu muttered.

In the main tent, Bison was pleased with the show and turned to the head of the Shadaloo Tong. "Ah, this is the life, eh, Sagat? To watch the girls dance, to breathe the night air, to mingle with fellow warriors."

But Sagat wasn't taken in. "Yes, thanks to you there are thousands of warriors in Shadaloo tonight: Enemies *you* brought to our shores when you took their citizens hostage."

"You fear a paper tiger," Bison replied with a dismissive wave of his hand. "With Colonel Guile dead, the democracies of the world will rattle their swords . . . and quietly slink away. Now on to business. I trust you have come prepared?"

Sagat snapped his fingers, and his men brought forth a dozen long, rectangular wooden boxes. Breaking one open, Sagat lifted out a field green automatic rifle with a large nightscope. Bison took the weapon from him, cocked it, and aimed through the scope.

"Excellent," Bison said. "With these the world will learn to fear me as much at night as they do during the day."

Sagat rolled his eyes impatiently. Would this blowhard never cease talking?

Bison handed the rifle back to Sagat's thug and turned to the head of the Shadaloo Tong.

"I am pleased with your goods, Sagat," he said grandly. "Now, as to payment. After I defeat the AN, what if I were to share the country with you?"

"When this war is over, we'll see how much of this country is left," Sagat replied dryly. "In the meantime, let's see the color of your money."

It was Bison's turn to snap his fingers. Several of his guards lugged strongboxes toward Sagat and opened them to reveal neat packets of $100 bills.

Sagat smiled.

But only for an instant.

There was something wrong with the money. Reaching down, he picked up a handful of the bills and inspected them.

Unbelievable!

Each one had Bison's portrait on it.

Eleven

Ken and Ryu reentered the tent just in time to see Sagat jump up from his seat and bellow, "Is this a joke!?"

The leader of the tong threw the bills at Bison. "This money isn't worth the paper it's printed on!"

The warlord reacted calmly, with the serene, undying confidence of a true madman. "On the contrary, every Bison dollar will soon be worth five British pounds."

Sagat stared at him like he was out of his mind. "How do you know that?"

"That is the exchange rate the Bank of England will set once I've kidnapped their queen," Bison informed him.

Ken glanced at Ryu and whispered, "Chun-Li said in ten minutes this whole place is going to be toast. This can't get any worse!"

"This conclave is over!" Viktor Sagat shouted. "I must have been insane to think I could do business with you, Bison. You're a raving lunatic."

Sagat grabbed a handful of the bills and threw them into a nearby fire.

Crack! Bison's massive hands crashed down on the table, smashing it in two. Finally the warlord had lost patience! He'd had enough of these insults!

In a flash, Sagat's thugs leaped to their feet and took

their leader's side. Bison's guards did the same.

Suddenly Ken and Ryu found themselves between the two groups of angry, trigger-happy men.

"I thought you said it couldn't get any worse," Ryu whispered, eyeing the savage men surrounding them.

"I was wrong," Ken admitted. "It just got worse, *a lot* worse."

WHAM! Up on the dais, Bison swept back his cape and unleashed a powerful blow.

WHAP! Sagat ducked and blocked it, then countered with one of his own.

BAM! SLAP! POW! SMACK! Like expert fencers who can't get past each other's defense, the two leaders punched and counterpunched. Meanwhile, their troops began to face off for one last cataclysmic marathon brawl . . . with Ken and Ryu caught in the middle!

"This doesn't look good," Ken whispered.

"That's an understatement," Ryu replied.

"Got any ideas?"

Ryu couldn't believe it. "How come I'm always the one who's supposed to come up with ideas? Why can't you ever come up with any?"

On both sides of them, groups of ferocious killers with blood in their eyes drew weapons and advanced.

"I've come up with plenty of ideas," Ken shot back. "Wasn't it my idea to sell the toy guns to Sagat?"

"Oh, yeah," Ryu nodded. "That was one of your truly great brainstorms."

"Hey, it almost worked," Ken sniffed.

"Well, *almost* doesn't cut it," Ryu said. "*Almost* doesn't get us champagne and caviar. *Almost* doesn't get us first-class plane tickets out of this mess. The only thing *almost* ever gets us is almost killed!"

Desperate for a way out, Ryu looked toward the stage. Honda and Balrog, still in their disguise of the "Benbelli Brothers," had just brought out a large, ornate Chinese box. Ryu had an idea. He turned to his partner.

"Back me up," he said, hissing.

Ken crossed his arms and shook his head. "Back yourself up," he replied with a pout.

"Don't quit on me now!" Ryu said, hissing again. "I've got an idea."

"Whoppee-do!" Ken was really peeved.

There was no time to waste. Ryu ran up onto the dais and got between Bison and Sagat.

Blam! He punched Bison as hard as he could in the jaw.

Despite himself, Ken rushed forward.

Wham! He delivered a crushing blow to Sagat.

The two powerful leaders stumbled backward in shock. A split second later, Ryu and Ken were surrounded by cocked weapons and glinting knives.

"How dare you interfere!" Bison roared.

"I had to, General," Ryu quickly explained. "You should not be fighting your great ally Sagat . . . not when Allied Nations spies are among us!"

"Where!?" Bison gasped.

Ryu pointed at the stage just as Honda and Balrog stepped into the Chinese box and pulled the door closed behind them. Bison, Sagat, and the others instantly rushed to the stage, but when Bison pulled open the door, the "Benbelli Brothers" had vanished!

In their place was a small video monitor. As they all watched, it crackled to life, showing a picture of Chun-Li. Beside her, Honda and Balrog were pulling off their Benbelli costumes. Behind all of them was a truck.

"Bison, Sagat," Chun-Li addressed them, "all of the weapons of death that you deal in are about to be blown sky-high. Too bad you're in the same tent with them."

As they all watched, Chun-Li nodded to Honda, who reached into the truck and released the emergency brake. The truck rolled away.

"Happy landings!" Balrog waved. Then he and the others disappeared into the dark.

Dee Jay poked his head around behind the monitor. "Uh, General, I'm pretty certain this is a live telecast."

Someone at the end of the tent parted the flaps. Now they could all see the truck bouncing and barreling toward them down a hill! Bison and the others looked back at the monitor, which also showed the truck careening toward them.

"What do we do?" Dee Jay asked.

"Change the channel!" Zangief suggested.

"Evacuate!" Bison shouted.

Everyone ran.

KA-BOOOOOOOOOOM! Chun-Li's truck, filled with crates of dynamite, smashed into two of Sagat's trucks filled with guns and ammunition. The explosion was so great that people were picked up and flung through the air like dolls. A huge mushroom cloud of flames rose into the sky, lighting up the jungle for miles in every direction.

"Oooof!" Ryu landed in some bushes.

"Ow!" Ken crashed to the ground near him.

Ryu got to his feet, dusted himself off, and helped up his partner.

"You okay?" Ryu asked.

"Oh, sure," Ken groaned. "Like every day I get blasted sixty feet through the air. Piece of cake."

Now two large figures near them picked themselves up off the ground. Bison and Sagat! Bison studied Ken and Ryu and then turned to the man he'd just been in hand-to-hand combat with.

"Sagat, are these men with you?" the warlord asked.

"Yes." Sagat nodded. Apparently the blast had knocked out whatever animosity the two men had for each other. "They're the ones who broke us out of prison."

Sagat pointed at Ken. "He killed Guile."

Bison looked impressed. He turned back to the tong leader and extended his hand. "Forgive me for my temper before, comrade."

Sagat hesitated, then shook it. Having made peace, they turned and stood together before the assembled throng of thugs and renegade soldiers. The crowd raised their fists, shouting, "Victory! Victory! Victory!"

Standing behind Bison and Sagat, Ken nudged Ryu with his elbow. "Nice going, dude."

"Hey, what did I do?" Ryu asked.

"You just doubled the size of Bison's army," Ken said. "If Guile wasn't already dead, this would kill him. I still don't understand why you had to warn that nut about the truck."

"I couldn't let Bison die here," Ryu said.

"Why not?" Ken asked. "It's as good a place as any to kill an insane, megalomaniac warlord."

"Listen," Ryu said, "if Bison died here, we might never find his fortress. We'd never find the hostages. I had to make sure he lived."

"Tell that to them." Ken nodded toward a clearing where Zangief and some of Bison's troopers appeared, dragging Chun-Li, Honda, and Balrog. The three had their hands tied behind their backs and were being pushed along roughly.

"They got caught!" Ryu gasped.

"Thanks to us," Ken said guiltily.

As Balrog, Honda, and Chun-Li were led past them, Chun-Li stared daggers at them.

"Hey, all's fair in love and war," Ryu said, trying to make it appear that he was still on Bison's side.

Chun-Li didn't answer. She just spit at him. The Bison troopers beside her laughed and dragged her away.

Twelve

The mood around the long wooden table in the AN headquarters was tense. Less than an hour before, the homing signal they'd all been waiting for had been picked up by an AN spy satellite high above Southeast Asia. It could only mean that Ken and Ryu had managed to reach Bison's fortress. Finally learning where the fortress was, Colonel Guile had immediately ordered his staff to formulate different attack plans for freeing the hostages.

Now Captain Sawada had just finished a lengthy presentation on the merits of an AN air attack, but it was clear that Colonel Guile wasn't happy.

"Thank you for that presentation, Captain," the colonel said, rising to his feet. "I'm afraid, however, that an air attack would result in horrendous casualties. You mustn't forget that Bison has extremely sophisticated ground-to-air weaponry. We know what North Korea, Iraq, and Libya have sold him. It's possible he's even got Patriot missiles."

"What else would you suggest doing to save the hostages?" Sawada asked.

"The only chance we have is an attack with a small amphibious force," Guile said.

"By water?" Sawada made a face. "That means going

up the Shadaloo River. Anyone crazy enough to do that would be a sitting duck."

"Unless you can squeeze under Bison's radar net," Guile said. "What we need is a single vessel equipped with stealth technology to go up the channel first and distract Bison's defenses. While they're distracted, the rest of the amphibious force goes in, riding as low as possible under the radar net."

"A single boat against everything Bison's got?" Sawada said, shaking his head. "The pilot would have to be out of his mind."

"Fortunately, Bison has driven me crazy," Guile said with a wry smile. He held up his watch. "I'm going to take the lead boat. Everyone synchronize watches. It's now oh-five-hundred. Castoff is at oh-six-hundred. Assemble your teams, gentlemen, this is it!"

It wasn't long before row after row of attack boats were lined up along the wharf. Standing in front of them were teams of troops in battle fatigues and light blue battle helmets, ready for action.

Guile, accompanied by Captain Sawada, stepped up to an outdoor lectern with a microphone to give the men their final orders. Guile was wearing a bulletproof battle vest. He was just about to begin the address when a long black limousine with fluttering AN flags on the fenders pulled up.

Guile recognized the car immediately. It belonged to the undersecretary-general of the Allied Nations. The limo stopped. The driver hopped out and opened the door for the undersecretary, a short, dignified-looking man with salt and pepper hair and wearing a dark suit.

The colonel turned away from the lectern and saluted stiffly. "Mr. Undersecretary, this is a surprise."

"As you were, Colonel," the undersecretary replied, casting a critical eye toward the troops waiting to board their boats.

"Welcome to the Shadaloo front," Guile said. "Your timing is perfect, sir. You're just in time to see the kickoff of the rescue mission to bring back the hostages."

The undersecretary studied Guile for a moment and then slowly shook his head. "I'm afraid not, Colonel. The AN Security Council has voted, and they've decided to negotiate."

"What!?" Guile was certain he must have heard wrong. The undersecretary *couldn't* have said that.

"They think they can deal with General Bison," the undersecretary explained. "We're all very appreciative of your efforts, but you are hereby instructed to call off the assault at once."

"And let the hostages be murdered?" Guile asked in disbelief.

"No," said the undersecretary. "You are to contact Bison and request an extension of the deadline."

"Oh, and I'm *sure* a madman like Bison will agree to that." Guile's words were heaped with sarcasm.

"He will when you tell him we are prepared to pay his ransom demand," the undersecretary said.

Guile stared at the man, not sure who was crazier, General Bison or the AN Security Council. "Excuse me, sir, but are you aware that the ransom demand is for twenty billion dollars?"

"We are."

"And has it occurred to anyone that if we cave in and pay the twenty billion, there's nothing that prevents Bison for taking more hostages next month and asking for fifty billion, and the month after that for a hundred billion? Heck, why stop there? Why not just ask for all the money in the world?"

The lines between the undersecretary's eyebrows deepened. "Colonel, have you lost your mind?"

"No," Guile replied, "but you've lost your guts."

The undersecretary's face hardened. "Colonel, you are hereby relieved of your command!"

Guile felt his blood start to boil. He spun around and grabbed the microphone off the lectern. "Soldiers," he announced, "I have just been given new orders. Our governments say the war is canceled. We can all go home."

Looks of shock and loud murmurs rippled through the assembled troops. But Guile wasn't finished yet.

"Yes, we can go home," he said, his words seething with fury. "Meanwhile, Bison gets rewarded for his crimes. And our friends and comrades who have already died here will have died for nothing. But we can all go home. Meanwhile, the ideals that brought us here . . . ideals like peace and freedom and justice . . . they get packed up along with our tents and our blankets. But we can all go home. . . ."

The robin's egg blue helmets shook back and forth. Not a soldier broke from the ranks.

"Well, I'm *not* going home!" Guile shouted. "I'm getting in my boat and I'm going upriver and I'm gonna kick that crazy warlord's butt so hard that the next Bison wannabe is gonna feel it! *Now, who here wants to go home? And who here wants to go with me?*"

The troops shouted and cheered, then turned for their boats. Guile turned and smiled politely at the undersecretary.

"Colonel Guile!" the man gasped. "This cannot be permitted! It's insubordination! You must stop them!"

"I'd love to, sir," Guile said with a shrug. "But I'm not in command anymore."

With that he turned and went to his boat.

Ryu and Ken stood in the command room of General Bison's fortress, staring at a map of the grounds displayed on the bank of video screens on the wall. Standing near them were Sagat, Vega, and other princes of the underworld.

"Look upon my works, ye mighty, and despair!" Bison cried with gleeful madness.

They had just been given a video tour of the fortress. Even Ryu had to admit he was impressed.

"You know, I'm starting to think this guy really *could* rule the world," Ken whispered.

"If all it took were guns and weaponry, I might have to agree," Ryu whispered back.

"Impressive, is it not?" Bison asked grandly. "You've just seen the best and most modern technology of both East and West. While their governments scorned me, their corporations adored me."

"Gee," Ken whispered to Ryu. "That's all I ever wanted, just to have a couple of large corporations adore me. Who needs girls?"

"Zangief," Bison ordered. "See that our new friends, Ken and Ryu, are given clean clothing."

"What a guy," Ryu mumbled.

"Hey, those red uniforms could catch on," Ken said. "Especially if Bison takes over the world."

Meanwhile, Bison turned to Sagat and his men. "Sagat, Vega, you are welcome to stay here. You may find the coming events most educational."

"What's he talking about?" Ken whispered.

"I think we're either gonna see Bison becoming a multibillionaire, or sixty-three hostages are gonna get fried," Ryu whispered back.

Just then they heard scuffling footsteps and the sounds of angry murmurs. A squad of Bison's men led Chun-Li, Honda, and Balrog into the room. They were all shackled, and their faces were bruised.

"What about these enemies of General Bison?" Zangief asked.

"Take those two to the interrogation room," Bison commanded, pointing at Honda and Balrog. "They will talk or they will die . . . preferably both."

The warlord turned and gazed at Chun-Li. A sinister smile appeared on his face. "Take the . . . *journalist* to my chambers. We have decided to grant her a . . . private interview."

"I understand, my General." Zangief grabbed her by the arm and started to lead her away past Ken and Ryu.

As Chun-Li passed them, her eyes raked them with hate. Ryu wished he could explain that things were not what they seemed, that the only reason he and Ken appeared to be on Bison's side was to get the homing device into the fortress so Guile could find it and save the hostages. But that would be impossible to explain. Chun-Li still thought Guile was dead.

The best Ryu could do was muster another weak smile.

Chun-Li responded by spitting at him again.

"You know," Ken said, "you keep that up and you're gonna get dehydrated."

Then Ken turned to his partner and whispered, "This sucks. They're good guys, like us."

"Lately I don't feel very good," Ryu muttered, glancing at the countdown clock. There were fewer than four hours before either the ransom money was paid, or the hostages were massacred one by one.

"So now what?" Ken asked.

Ryu looked down at his tattered, dirty clothes. "Like the boss says, I guess we get new duds."

One of the guards led them down a corridor to a barracks area that sort of reminded Ryu of a locker room. They were instructed to throw their old clothing into a disposal hatch, where it was quickly incinerated in a ball of orange flame. Then they showered and changed into red and white karate robes with the silver Bison insignia on the breast.

"Ah." Ken smiled and combed his wet hair. "I feel like a million bucks."

"If you felt like twenty billion, we could ransom the hostages," Ryu quipped. "So now what?"

They looked around the room and noticed that the guard who'd escorted them to the barracks was gone.

"Guess we're on our own," Ken said.

"Let's take a walk," said Ryu.

They started out of the barracks and passed savage-looking Bison troopers coming in. Ken grinned and kept up a steady banter. "Hey, how're you doing? . . . Nice gun you got there. . . . Long live Bison."

Turning to Ryu, he whispered, "I'm getting tired of this."

"Why?" Ryu asked. "You're a natural lowlife."

"Hey, lowlife's better than *no* life." Ken said. "The sooner we escape, the better. Did you happen to get a good look at that video map of this place?"

"Just the left side," Ryu said.

"Good, 'cause I got the right side," Ken said. "Let's go."

"Where?"

"Get Honda and Balrog before the torturer turns them into hamburger," Ken said.

"I thought you wanted to escape," Ryu said.

"I do," Ken answered. "And after we save their butts Honda and Balrog are gonna help us find the exit!"

They headed down a side corridor, then down a stairs toward the dungeon.

Balrog had been in a lot of tight squeezes before. It was the sort of thing that came with the territory. But he couldn't remember a time when things looked as bleak as they did right now. He and Honda were in a dungeon under the fortress, a place that made him feel as if he'd just stepped back a thousand years in time.

Chained to an ancient stone wall by his wrists and feet, he could feel the cold dampness of the rock at his back. Except for a huge rough-hewn wooden door and some tiny barred windows, the room was lined with stone. It was gloomy, dank, and smelled of centuries of sweat and terror. A pile of old human skulls lay in one corner, covered with cobwebs.

Whap! A few feet away, a tall, bulky torturer in black clothes whipped a rattan cane against Honda's back. Honda was locked in some kind of ancient wooden rack. Balrog winced at the sound and the imagined agony his buddy must be in. But Honda hardly blinked. Balrog couldn't imagine how he could stand the pain.

Whap! The torturer brought the cane down on the sumo's back again. Balrog grimaced. Maybe Honda wasn't showing it, but he had to be suffering mightily inside. Balrog felt his stomach twist and growl from a combination of hunger and anxiety.

Whap! Balrog wanted to scream out and tell the torturer to stop. If words could kill, he would gladly use them now.

Then, miraculously, the torture did stop. Huffing and puffing from exertion, the torturer came toward Balrog.

"You are next, Yankee," he gasped, trying to catch his breath.

"Maybe you ought to lie down and take a rest first," Balrog suggested.

Smack! The torturer punched him hard in the face. Then he turned and left the room.

Balrog winced as his friend's eyes met his. Long, ugly slashes and bloody, swollen red welts rose off Honda's back.

"Where do you think he went?" Honda asked.

"I don't know," Balrog said. "Maybe he actually decided to take my advice."

"Or maybe he just went to find something that would do the job a little faster," Honda said.

The dungeon grew quiet. Balrog looked at Honda, but he could no longer see his friend's face. Honda kept his head hung. He seemed to be breathing slowly.

"Hey, Ed," Balrog said softly.

"Hmmm?"

"You okay?"

"I guess."

"That guy was a total sadist," Balrog said. "How'd you keep from crying out?"

"I'm sumo," Honda said between labored breaths. "My body can be in one place. My mind, in another."

"Well, next time your mind leaves," Balrog said, "tell it to bring back a pizza."

Honda smirked and then turned to his friend. Balrog

could see the pain in his eyes. "Listen. If he starts on me again I . . . I don't know if I can take much more."

Balrog nodded. He knew it had taken a lot for Honda to admit that. He had to do something. He didn't know what, but something. He looked around the dungeon. There were plenty of things he could use, if only he could reach them! But as long as he was chained to the wall in this ancient dungeon . . .

Wait a minute!

Ancient . . . that was it. The manacles that held him to the wall were anchored in four spots, one behind each foot and each hand. Pulling at all four equally, he didn't have a chance of breaking free.

But maybe if he just concentrated on one . . .

Concentrating all his might, grunting and grimacing as hard as he could, he started to pull against the chain holding his right hand.

"What are you doing?" Honda asked.

"What does it look like?" Balrog replied with a grunt.

"Forget it," Honda said. "These things have been in that wall for a thousand years."

"Yeah, that's sort of what I'm hoping," Balrog replied.

But the chain holding his right hand wouldn't give. Finally Balrog gave up, exhausted by the effort.

"Save your strength, my friend," Honda warned him. "You'll need it later."

But Balrog was certain they had a better chance now than later. Pausing until he'd regained his strength, he started to pull against the chain holding his left hand.

"Balrog, you're crazy." Honda sounded worried.

Wedging his elbow against the cold stone wall, Balrog gave it all the strength he had. But once again, it wasn't enough. He flopped back against the wall, his chest heaving for breath.

"Hey, I appreciate the effort," Honda said.

Balrog nodded, but inside he knew he had to do it. Just trying wouldn't help his friend. He had to succeed.

Wait a minute!

Balrog reached his right hand out as far as the chain would allow.

Honda looked up at him curiously. "Now what?"

"Grab my hand," Balrog said.

"Why?"

"Just do it!"

"Hey, this isn't a Nike commercial?"

"Someday you'll have to explain to me how you can make jokes in a situation like this," Balrog said. "But right now, if you don't grab my hand you're gonna have to face whatever that guy comes back in here with."

"You just convinced me," Honda said, reaching out and grasping Balrog's right hand with his left.

"Okay, now pull!" Balrog said, grunting.

The two men strained against the chain holding Balrog's right hand to the wall. Their muscles bulged, and sweat dripped down their faces. Their hands throbbed.

But they kept at it until . . . *crunk!*

With a small cloud of dust, the chain pulled out of the wall.

The effort left them both exhausted. Their arms hung limp for a moment as they caught their breaths.

"You should've told me you had Wheaties for breakfast," Honda said with a wink.

With his right arm free, Balrog now went to work on the manacle holding his left hand.

Crunk! Now that one gave way as well.

"My hero." Honda sighed and batted his eyelashes.

"You just better hope I get my legs free before that torturer comes back," Balrog said, straining all his might against the chains holding his right leg.

It wasn't long before Balrog had pulled himself free of the wall. Freeing Honda was simple. Balrog found a metal bar and pried the big man's manacles from the rack.

"Way to go, bro." Honda and Balrog exchanged high fives.

"Now let's blow this joint." Balrog turned to go but suddenly stopped. He could hear the sound of scuffling in the hallway outside the dungeon, then footsteps.

"Someone's coming," Honda said with a hiss.

Balrog quickly reached down and picked up a length of loose chain. Honda did the same. Then they hid behind the large wooden door.

A moment later the door creaked open and Ryu and Ken peeked in.

Whoosh! Two necklaces of chain whipped through the air and caught each man by the throat. Balrog and Honda pulled hard on the chains, strangling Ryu and Ken and instantly bringing them to their knees.

"Well, look who it is!" Balrog said gleefully. "Our little buddies who double-crossed us."

Ryu and Ken gasped for breath. Their lungs were burning, and their necks felt like they were about to snap.

"Wegh-hon-degh-hame-chide!" Ken managed to utter, gasping.

Balrog looked at Honda and frowned. "What'd he say?"

"I think he said, 'Hail to M. Bison,' " Honda said.

"These guys must be double agents."

"Crazy fanatics," Balrog muttered and choked Ken harder.

"Wegh-hon-degh-hame-chide!" Ken just barely managed to say again with a gasp.

"You know what?" Balrog said. "I think he's saying he can lead us outside."

"You think?" Honda asked.

Ken and Ryu's faces had turned as red as tomatoes. Their eyes were bulging. Ryu's field of vision was starting to narrow as he slipped into unconsciousness.

"Let him go and see," Balrog said.

Honda let Ken go. The American street fighter slumped to the floor, gasping for breath.

"Did you say you could lead us outside?" Honda asked.

"No," Ken replied, gasping again. "I said, 'We're on the *same side*.' "

Thirteen

Chun-Li burned with hatred and humiliation as she stood in Bison's private quarters, staring up at a huge portrait of the man she despised over all others in the world. The painting showed Bison on a bucking stallion with his hand in the air and reminded her of one she'd once seen of Napoleon.

Chun-Li would have ripped the painting off the wall, but her hands were tied behind her with leather straps. Bison's acolytes had dressed her in a sheer red dress with a high slit, like the ones geisha girls wore. Other Bison aides had applied heavy white and red makeup to her face and had parted her black hair in the middle, creating two braids that were coiled and pinned on the sides of her head. Apparently this was how Bison liked his women — painted, helpless, and tied up.

Chun-Li glanced around the room. It was a monument to an egomaniacal madman, from the ornate chandelier made of human bones to the furniture all designed in the style of the winged insignia Bison was so fond of.

A door behind her opened, and the renegade general himself stepped in.

"Ah, I see you appreciate fine art," Bison said.

Chun-Li glared at him. "I would, if there were any around here."

Bison only smiled and removed his hat. "You seem to be very angry with me. You ridicule me, you tried to kill me. Why?"

"Because I hate you." Chun-Li practically spat the words out.

"Such strong feelings." Bison undid his cape and hung it up.

"Why? We've never met."

"Twenty years ago," Chun-Li said icily. "I was a girl living in a small village just over the Chinese border. You were just another petty drug lord. You hadn't promoted yourself to 'general' yet."

"Then it was quite a while ago," Bison said with a nod as he unsnapped his shoulder armor.

"You and your gang of murderers gathered your ounce of courage to raid across the border," Chun-Li said. "You needed food, weapons, slave labor for your fields of poppies and hemp. My father was the village magistrate. He had once been a respected judge in Beijing, but the Red Guards had forced him out. He was a simple man who brought the village a simple code: justice.

"When he heard you were coming, he gathered the few people he could to stand against you. And they won. You and your bullies were turned back by simple farmers with axes and pitchforks."

Bison shrugged as he undid the metal gauntlets covering his forearms and set them down on a table.

"My father saved his village," Chun-Li went on. "But it was at the cost of his own life. You had him shot as you ran away. You were a hero at a thousand paces."

Bison pulled on a maroon smoking jacket and tied it at the waist. He pressed a button on the wall, and two doors parted, revealing a hidden bar. He poured drinks into two metal flagons, each decorated with the silver Bison insignia. He stirred them with plastic swizzle sticks molded in the same design.

"I'm sure you remember it quite well," Chun-Li said.

But Bison shook his head. "Sorry, I don't remember any of it."

"You don't?" Chun-Li was stunned.

"For you, the day Bison graced your village was the most important day of your life," the renegade general said pompously. "For me . . . it was a Tuesday."

Chun-Li could hardly contain her fury. Across the room, Bison reclined on a sofa and sipped his drink.

"So this is how you've spent your life?" Bison asked. "Seeking revenge?"

"I spent the past ten years in the media world," Chun-Li said. "I used my credentials to gather intelligence. I found partners who hated you and your friends as much as I did."

"The sumo and the boxer." Bison swirled the ice cubes in his drink and took another sip. Then he turned to an elaborate music system and turned on some slow mood music. The lights around the room dimmed.

"Most importantly," Chun-Li said, "I studied the martial arts of three continents, learning to kill in a thousand ways so that one day I could avenge my father and put an end to your reign of terror myself."

"I don't think so." Bison shook his head with an amused smile. "I have spies everywhere. No one has ever seen you in combat. You've always hid behind your two powerful friends. Why, I know for a fact that since you have entered this country you have not thrown a single punch."

Chun-Li watched silently as he stretched out and relaxed. "Let me tell you something, my dear. I know women. And *you* are harmless."

"That is exactly what I wanted you to think," Chun-Li replied.

Bison smiled at her.

Chun-Li smiled back. *"Ya-tai!"* she screamed.

Snap! In a clean, deft move she broke the leather straps binding her wrists behind her back.

Startled by her show of hidden strength, Bison started to rise from the couch.

"Ya-chi!" Fists clenched, legs extended, Chun-Li launched herself at him in an impressive display of martial perfection.

Wham! She kicked the general so hard in the chest that he was driven back into the sofa, cracking the frame in half.

Bison tumbled to the floor in an explosion of splinters and upholstery. Chun-Li landed beside him in a graceful roll. Bison started to pull himself up.

Whack! Chun-Li caught him in the side of the head with a powerful spin kick.

Crash! The kick drove Bison headfirst into his bar, shattering the glasses and bottles. Stunned by the dual blows, the general sagged against the wall. Chun-Li closed in for the death blow. Twenty years of hate and anger pulsed through her. She was a split second away from fulfilling a lifelong murderous dream.

"Chun-Li, don't do it!" a voice shouted.

Chun-Li spun around. Coming through the doorway were Ken, Ryu, Balrog, and Honda.

"Honda, Balrog," she said with a gasp. "What are you doing with those traitors? They betrayed us!"

"No, they're on our side," Balrog said.

"Li, listen to them," Honda begged.

"No!" Chun-Li spun around to finish the job she'd started. "He has to die for his crimes!"

"Kill him and you kill all the hostages," Ryu said.

"He's right," Ken added. "We need Bison alive. He's the only one who can give the order to release the hostages."

For a second, Chun-Li was frozen with indecision. That was all the time Bison needed. He rolled away into an alcove and pressed a red button on the wall.

Whoosh! A glass wall suddenly dropped from the ceiling, separating Bison from the street fighters. Doors around the room began to click as they locked.

Thunk! Chun-Li hurtled herself against the glass wall, but she only bounced off.

Hiisssss! Ryu and the others looked up just as yellow gas began to pour out of vents in the ceiling above them.

"Ha!" Muffled by the glass, Bison laughed as the street fighter gasped, staggered, and crumpled to the floor.

Fourteen

With Colonel Guile's stealth boat in the lead, the squadron of AN attack boats swept upriver in a V formation. Cammy and T. Hawk accompanied Guile in his boat, monitoring the weaponry and navigational equipment.

Cammy stared at the screen with alarm. "Colonel, aircraft approaching on our six!"

"Friendly or enemy?" Guile asked.

Before Cammy could answer, the radio crackled on. "Colonel Guile! Colonel Guile, you are ordered to acknowledge!"

Guile grabbed the mike. "Who is this?"

"This is the undersecretary," the radio replied. "I am above you in the helicopter. This is your last chance to turn around, Colonel Guile. Return to the base at once or face court-martial!"

Guile rolled his eyes and glanced at T. Hawk. "You believe this guy?"

"Uh, sir, in roughly ninety seconds that chopper is going to hit Bison's radar perimeter," T. Hawk replied nervously. "As soon as they pick him up, our sneak attack is blown."

"Great." Guile groaned and shook his head.

"Colonel Guile"—the radio crackled again—"I order

you to turn around immediately, or so help me, I'll have you shot!"

Guile could see it again. Those idiot bureaucrats and politicians—complete chickens—forcing him to back down, as they did in Bosnia. No way, not this time. Guile held the microphone up to his lips.

"You'll have *me* shot?" He laughed. "In approximately one minute your chopper is going to enter Bison's radar perimeter and he's gonna blow you to bits . . . and if he misses, *I'll* finish the job for him."

"You're bluffing," the undersecretary said over the radio.

That was it. "T. Hawk, take the controls." Guile handed the boat over to his aide and climbed in back. He grabbed a flare gun from the bulkhead and pushed open the cockpit.

The wind whipped around his head as the boat roared up the river, with the helicopter hovering fifty yards above it. Guile aimed the flare as close as he could to the helicopter and fired. The bright orange flare burst out of the gun and shot upward toward the chopper's windshield.

Ooops! Guile couldn't help grinning. The flare had gotten a little closer than he'd wanted. In a flash, the chopper veered away. Guile waved and pulled the hatch closed.

As he climbed back into the driver's seat, T. Hawk handed over the boat's controls. Meanwhile, the undersecretary's voice blared over the radio again.

"Darn you, Guile! You've got no respect for authority! Just wait until I—"

Click. Guile turned the radio off.

T. Hawk gave Guile a sidelong glance. "Uh, excuse me

for saying this, sir, but that was our boss."

"Hey, he fired me," Guile replied. "He's just lucky I don't work for the post office."

Cammy tapped him on the shoulder. "Approaching attack vector Alpha, sir."

"Okay." Guile picked up the radio and switched frequencies. "Attention all boats: Stand by at attack vector Alpha. I'll take out the enemy radar. Captain Sawada?"

"Yes, sir," Sawada's voice came over the radio.

"I'm counting on you," Guile said.

"Don't worry, we'll be there, Colonel," Sawada assured him. "Just promise me you'll save some butts for us to kick."

"That's a promise." Guile smiled and turned off the radio. Behind him, the entire formation of boats veered off, leaving Guile's boat alone to venture forth up the murky river. Guile and his crew braced themselves for the teeth-jarring vibration that came as he switched the craft into stealth mode. There was a violent lurch, and then the special surface of the boat hummed and glowed. Chameleonlike, it changed colors with the passing landscape. To the human eye, it was almost invisible. And—more importantly—to any electronic eyes or ears, it was completely invisible.

As they raced upriver with jungle on both sides, T. Hawk and Cammy exchanged concerned looks. It was a lonely feeling, racing into the jaws of the enemy alone. Guile looked up at a snapshot he'd taped to the dashboard. It showed him with Charlie Blanka and those two crazy French girls Darcy and Jeri, back in Paris after Bosnia. What a great time they'd had. Friends like Charlie Blanka were rare.

Don't worry, buddy, Guile thought. *I'm coming. And I'm going to keep coming until I've found you.*

But the Charlie Blanka Guile knew in Paris no longer existed. Instead, now seated in the brainwashing chamber was a creature as powerful as it was terrifying. Barely recognizable as a human, he had enormous muscle mass and the lightning reflexes of a cheetah. The DNA mutagens had turned his skin green and his hair orange. His eyes were white, and his canine teeth had grown into fangs.

Almost all memory of his life as Carlos Blanka, soldier, had been erased. It was now being replaced with the visual images of destruction and mayhem Bison had ordered Dr. Dhalsim to brainwash him with. As if to make it even more painful, the very images to be downloaded passed across the screen for the doctor to witness first.

As each moment passed, the thought of what he had done weighed more and more heavily on Dr. Dhalsim. The idea that all his research, all his work, was resulting in the creation of a beast of mass destruction became almost unbearable. Was this the way he wanted to be remembered? As the Dr. Frankenstein of the twentieth century?

Dhalsim glanced over at the guard assigned to watch him. The man was engrossed in a girlie magazine. With a casual flick of his finger, the doctor hit a control on the computer console. The visual images vanished. The words CEREBRAL DOWNLOAD HALTED 49 PERCENT appeared on the screen.

Keeping one eye on the guard, Dhalsim quickly typed new commands—commands he had secretly programmed behind Bison's back weeks earlier. Now, another set of words appeared on the computer screen: ALTERNATE CEREBRAL PROGRAMMING ON-LINE. BEGIN DOWNLOAD.

What happened next brought tears to Dhalsim's eyes. Before him on the monitor passed pictures of great acts of decency, kindness, and giving, scenes of people helping each other, nursing each other, building, sacrificing, and uniting. Scenes of weddings, happy children, porpoises swimming gracefully in the sea. The faces of Dhalsim's heroes—Florence Nightingale, Gandhi, Martin Luther King Jr., Nelson Mandela, and Mother Teresa — now floated like angels across the screen.

Inside the tank, Blanka at first appeared puzzled by the sudden change. Then slowly, almost painfully, a smile appeared on his lips.

Dhalsim blinked back the tears and glanced at the computer terminal. The ALTERNATE DOWNLOAD screen flashed 65 PERCENT . . . 70 PERCENT . . . 75 PERCENT. . . .

Dhalsim held his breath. The mutant beast in the chamber would never be 100 percent good. He had already been programed with too much violence and madness. But Dhalsim knew that if he could complete the alternate download, the beast would have more good than bad in him. And *that* could make a difference.

"What are you doing there?" The sound of the guard's voice made Dhalsim jump. He leaned over the console, trying to block the guard's view of the monitor.

"Uh, nothing," he stammered.

Zap! A bolt from the guard's electric prod doubled the scientist over.

The guard stared down at the monitor, and his eyes went wide. He yanked a walkie-talkie from his belt and started to yell. "Security! This is the la—"

Clang! Dhalsim crept up behind the man and smacked an empty metal canister down on his head. The guard staggered, and the walkie-talkie went flying.

Whamp! The guard angrily backhanded Dhalsim, sending the scientist backward until he slammed into a wall and crumpled to the ground.

The guard stormed over to him and grabbed him by the neck, yanking him up. "Think you're smart, do you?" the guard yelled, tightening his grip around Dhalsim's neck. "Let's see how smart you are when you're not breathing!"

Dhalsim struggled with all his strength. The two men twisted and churned in a dance of death, smashing into tables and knocking over beakers and vials.

Some of the DNA mutagens splashed on Dhalsim. Oddly, Dhalsim wondered if he would live long enough for it to affect him. But by then the guard was pushing him up against the computer console. His hands were still around the doctor's throat. Dhalsim was weakening quickly as the breath and life were choked out of him. He reached out desperately, trying to hit switches and buttons on the console in one last-ditch effort.

Click! He hit the one he needed.

Behind them, the doors of the brainwashing chamber hissed open and a thick cloud of vapor poured out. Blanka was free to leave. Dhalsim had no idea if he'd done the right thing. If the monster was evil, then there was little left on earth to stop Bison from using him to conquer the planet.

The light began to grow dim in Dhalsim's eyes. His lungs throbbed painfully and screamed for air. But it was too late. . . . He was fading. . . .

Ahhhhhhhhhh! There was a sudden, bloodcurdling scream. Dhalsim felt the hands around his neck go limp. But it was too late. The scientist slipped into unconsciousness.

Fifteen

Ryu felt like he was dreaming in slow motion. His thoughts were as thick and gooey as cake frosting. His eyes opened but couldn't focus. He didn't know where he was. That yellow gas was nasty stuff. All he knew was what he could feel. He was lying on some kind of metal catwalk, his wrists handcuffed to a railing. Others were handcuffed around him.

He slowly struggled to his feet. His vision was coming back. He and the other street fighters were handcuffed to the rail at the back of Bison's command center. Across the room from them was the huge bank of video screens. Dozens of Bison troopers and technicians milled about. On the floor below, Bison looked up at his prisoners. Vega and Sagat stood beside him.

"I told you we couldn't trust them," Vega was saying to Sagat as he glared at Ryu and his companions.

Bison had the benign smile of someone who is certain of victory. "Vega, be civil," he said. "They worked so hard to get here. Let them enjoy their ringside seats."

The renegade general stepped closer to the street fighters. Ryu watched as Honda, Balrog, Chun-Li, and Ken came to their senses and stood up unsteadily, blinking as if they were in shock.

"You know, it's interesting," Bison called up to them

from the floor below. "Had you worked together as a team instead of against each other, you might have been successful. There's a lesson in cooperation here. Too bad you won't live to learn from it."

Bison might have continued the lecture, but Dee Jay suddenly called to him. "General! Something strange on the river. Our radar stations are failing—and in sequence!"

Bison quickly turned and headed for the radar console. Vega and Sagat followed him. Now Zangief approached the street fighters.

"Ryu, Ken," he said indignantly, "General Bison is great man who only wants peace and happiness for whole world. Why you betray him?"

Ken stared at him in disbelief. "Come on, Zangief, wake up and smell the coffee!"

Zangief scowled as if he didn't understand. "Coffee? Where is coffee?"

"No, megabrains, that's just a saying," Ken said.

Zangief frowned. Then he grinned as if struck by a sudden insight. "Ah! Now I understand! It is because I take your women! You are mad with me."

Ken glanced at Ryu and rolled his eyes. "How could anyone be *that* dumb?" he whispered.

"Hey," Ryu whispered back. "He believes in Bison, doesn't he?"

A siren rang out, and lights began to flash around the command center. A voice coming over a speaker shouted, "Battle stations! Code One!"

Meanwhile, Bison was still hunched over the radar console, trying to make sense of a tactical display. Everything said the river was empty. Yet, the radar perimeter was crashing, beacon by beacon, one by one.

Suddenly Bison brightened. "Of course!" he exclaimed. "A stealth attack boat! Coming upriver alone! Dee Jay, activate sonar detectors and filter all inputs!"

"Yes, sir!" Dee Jay's fingers raced over the computer controls.

The street fighters' eyes widened as a huge image of Guile's stealth boat appeared on the bank of video screens.

"Prepare for attack mode!" Bison shouted.

Ryu felt a chill run through him. The approaching boat was their salvation, but he feared they were about to see it destroyed.

On the bank of screens, they watched as hatches on either side of the stealth attack boat opened and rotating guns began to fire toward the riverbanks.

"What're they doing?" Ken whispered.

"Got me." Ryu shook his head. From his point of view, the guns seemed to be firing aimlessly into the jungle.

"No," Chun-Li said with a hiss. "Look: radar!"

Now Ryu saw what she was talking about. Set deep in the jungle were the large red sweeping radar outposts that served as beacons in Bison's defense system. Suddenly a radar installation vanished in an explosion of red fire.

"Whoever's in that boat is trying to knock them out," Balrog whispered. At the same moment a second radar installation blew apart.

"It's a suicide mission!" Ryu said with a gasp, struck by the courage of the person who would single-handedly subject himself or herself to every weapon Bison had.

"Perimeter guns, fire!" Bison shouted.

Rising out of the jungle were massive guns that fired

by remote control. Out on the river, the stealth boat weaved in evasive action, but bullets raked its gunwales and ricocheted off its windows.

Bison lifted his microphone. "Attention attack boat: This is General Bison. Our defenses are locked on you. Identify yourself!"

"This is the collection agency, Bison," a voice replied. "Your butt is six months overdue. And it's mine."

"That's Guile!" Chun-Li said with a gasp.

"What?" Sagat asked, startled. "Guile? Alive?"

"It's a trick!" Vega yelled.

"You wish!" Ken yelled from the catwalk.

Bison studied Ken and then smiled.

"Yes, of course." Bison turned to Sagat. "His death was designed to ingratiate his spies with you. How else would you take them in? Very clever."

The warlord turned back to the screen. "Your faked death was quite convincing, Guile. But this time, Colonel, you will die for real."

Ryu and the others watched as Bison stepped calmly onto his floating platform and rose into the air in the middle of the control room to get a better view of the screen.

"Activate all underwater mines!" he shouted. "For *my* command!"

On the screens, the image of the boat was replaced by tactical computer graphics showing the hidden river mines. Each mine was as large as a giant pumpkin and covered with detonation spikes. The screens divided in half. One half showed the position of the mines relative to Guile's boat. The other showed the boat itself, still racing upriver.

As the boat neared the first mines, Bison detonated

them. On the video screen, huge white geysers of water burst out of the surface as the mines exploded, rocking the boat like a plastic toy in someone's bathtub.

Boom! Boom! Boom! One after another, the mines exploded. The whole scene reminded Ryu of some kind of giant computer game, with Bison controlling the action. As the stealth attack boat raced farther and farther upstream, the mines were massed more tightly until . . .

KA-BOOM! The boat exploded into a fireball, throwing burning debris in every direction for hundreds of yards. Suddenly the entire videobank was nothing but fire. The street fighters watched in stunned silence.

His face lit red by the video fire, Bison turned to them and raised a triumphant fist. "Game . . . over!" he cried.

The reeds near the edge of the river quietly parted as three wet but very much alive commandos crawled up the riverbank. Knowing that Bison had them in a radar lock, Guile, Cammy, and T. Hawk had jumped from the stealth attack boat just moments before Bison had blown it up.

Now they crept up onshore in the underbrush a hundred yards from the ancient temple that covered Bison's fortress. T. Hawk wore a battle vest loaded with C-4 plastic explosives. Cammy carried a thick coil of rope over her shoulder. Guile crouched in the tall grass and brush and gazed up at the crumbling pile of stones used as a place of peaceful worship for thousands of years.

"What do you think?" Cammy whispered to him.

"I never would have guessed Bison would pick a place like this," Guile whispered back.

"Sort of ironical," T. Hawk quipped.

"Not to a man who thinks he's a god," Guile said.

T. Hawk nodded gravely and pointed toward the base of the ruins. "If he's a god, those must be his angels."

Guile looked ahead and saw three Bison guards with red helmets and silver face masks.

"I can take those three," he said. "You follow behind me and take care of anyone who may be attracted by the noise."

Guile crept up through the brush and trees. The three guards stopped to light cigarettes. Guile picked up a coconut and lofted it silently in the air.

Thunk! The coconut hit the ground just past the men. Just as Guile hoped, they turned toward the sound, raising their guns.

Wham! Pow! Whack! With swift whirling kicks, Guile blindsided the three men in rapid succession. As he expected, the commotion brought several more of Bison's men running, but Cammy and T-Hawk quickly and quietly brought them down.

As soon as they were all taken care of, Guile led Cammy and T-Hawk to the base of the temple. A large steel door at the entrance was locked shut.

"How do we get in?" Cammy asked with a gasp, still breathing hard from the fight.

"I'll set some charges, sir," T. Hawk said, pulling several packets of C-4 plastic explosive from his battle vest. "We can crack this can in no time."

"No." Guile raised his hand to stop him. "We don't want to announce ourselves just yet."

"How else are we gonna get in?" T. Hawk asked.

Guile looked around. "They have to breathe down there. Let's find a ventilation shaft."

It wasn't long before they found what they were looking for—a large piece of metal grating covering a hole in the ground. Unfortunately, a rather large black snake had also found it and was resting on the metal grating.

"Uh, after you, sir." T. Hawk swallowed.

Guile knelt down and gently lifted the grate over the ventilation shaft. The snake slithered away through the tall, wild grass. T. Hawk peered down.

"This isn't a ventilation shaft, it's an old well," he whispered.

"Then you can bet a ventilation shaft runs into it somewhere down there," Guile said.

"How are we going to find it?" Cammy asked.

The three of them looked at each other. One of them had to go down.

"Okay, Cammy, give me the rope," Guile said. "You two set the markers."

They lashed one end of the rope to a tree and then Guile backed quietly into the well and started to rappel down. The rocky walls were slippery and damp. Old tree roots stuck out here and there, and moisture dripped down the walls. As Guile descended deeper into the darkness, the square patch of sunlight above him grew smaller and smaller.

"Colonel," Cammy called down after a few minutes, "electronic and visual markers have been set!"

"Good," Guile called back up.

"ETA landing zone in twelve minutes," Cammy said.

"Roger, Lieutenant, I'll be ready." No sooner were the words out of his mouth than a large tarantula hopped off the cistern wall onto his shoulder. Guile lost his grip on the rope and slid nearly twenty feet before he regained control.

I'll be ready, he thought. *If I live!*

Finally he came to another metal grating in the wall of

the well. Just as he'd expected, modern metal ductwork led away horizontally. Guile kicked off from the wall and swung back on the rope.

Clang! He kicked in the grating and crawled into the duct. Now he just had to hope it didn't lead straight into Bison's command center.

Guile pulled out a gun and a flashlight and crawled on his hands and knees. The air in the duct was oddly cold and damp, making him wonder if it was running from an air-conditioned computer center.

A little while later he pushed through another grate and climbed up through the floor of the darkened laboratory. Guile stood up and looked slowly around. Lit only by emergency lighting, it appeared that a fight had taken place there recently.

The gruesomely mangled body of a Bison guard lay on the floor, the eyes frozen open in terror, the neck broken, the limbs twisted into unnatural positions. The colonel had seen the horrors of combat many times in his life, but he was sure he'd never seen anything like this. Only something inhumanely powerful could have done it.

Guile stepped forward through the shadows with great caution. Here and there, shorted electric wires flickered and sizzled. The flashlight beam picked up something large and white. It looked like some sort of underwater chamber with round windows. Inside was a seat with all sorts of electronic gear and dripping IVs. Guile felt a sickening chill. He'd never seen such a thing before, but it looked disturbingly like a torture or brainwashing chamber.

He glanced back at the battered body of the guard and wondered if the two things had something in common.

114

And then he sensed something move behind him.

Guile quickly spun, but it was two late. The thing grabbed him and lifted him effortlessly off the ground.

Wham! Guile felt the hard, unforgiving wall of concrete smash against his back. The blow nearly knocked him unconscious. For the first time in his life, he knew he was in the grip of something against which he didn't have a chance.

Sixteen

*W*ham! Grunting and snarling, the thing smashed Guile into the wall again. At first glance, Guile couldn't believe what he was looking at. Its features were only vaguely human. Long orange hair spread back from the thick, pinched features of its face. It was hunched over with muscle mass like Guile had never seen before. The way it picked him up, he might just as well have been a toy soldier.

Wham! Again Guile was smashed into the wall and again he looked down at his attacker. There was something incredibly, bizarrely familiar. . . .

Charlie? It didn't seem possible.

But Bison had taken Blanka, along with the hostages.

The creature was just about to smash Guile into the wall again. Guile doubted he'd survive another blow. He had only one chance.

"Carlos?" he said with a grunt. "Carlos, is that you?"

The creature suddenly hesitated. Its face twisted as if a primitive mind inside was at work. Guile didn't know whether to be happy or horrified. Could it really be his friend?

"Charlie, it's me, William."

Guile felt the creature's grip on him loosen. He felt himself set down on the ground. Then it *was* Charlie.

116

Guile felt a surge of rage and horror inside. How had Bison done this to his best friend?

"Wi . . . William?" the creature struggled with the words like a child just learning to speak.

"I'm your friend," Guile said.

"F . . . friend," Blanka repeated.

Guile had never felt so devastated in his life. "How?" he whispered, gasping, "What did they do to you?"

"To me . . ." Blanka grunted, as if only now realizing what he was and who he had been.

Guile watched in tormented amazement as the huge, powerful creature sank miserably to the floor, holding pathetically on to his friend's leg.

"Help me, William," Blanka whispered desperately. "Please help me."

Guile knew what his friend was asking for. He wanted to be put out of his misery. He wanted Guile to kill him. Guile put his hand gently on Blanka's head. "Yes, Carlos. I . . . I'll try to help you."

It was the hardest thing Guile had ever had to do, but somehow he managed to draw his pistol and cock it. Rage coursed through his veins. He would help his friend . . . and then he would make Bison pay!

He started to aim the pistol down at the creature's head. He hated this! He would make Bison suffer for doing this to his friend.

His finger started to close around the trigger.

"Good-bye, my friend. . . ."

"Stop!" From out of nowhere, a hand closed over the gun.

Guile looked up into the face of Dr. Dhalsim.

"You have no right," the scientist said.

Guile's jaw clenched tightly. Then slowly he turned,

aiming the gun at Dhalsim. "Who are you?"

"Dhalsim. Dr. Dhalsim."

"Tell me something, Dr. Dhalsim," Guile said. "Did you do this to my friend?"

Dhalsim looked down at Blanka, then back at Guile and nodded. "Yes. I was part of this nightmare."

"Then I have the right," Guile said, squeezing the trigger slowly, "to kill *you*."

To Guile's surprise, the scientist nodded. "Yes, you may. I'm guilty, and I regret what I've done terribly. But let me explain something to you first so that you'll understand. Otherwise you'll go through your life wondering how this horrible thing happened."

Guile kept the gun aimed at the scientist's forehead. "You better talk fast, Dr. Dhalsim. I don't have much time."

Dhalsim explained how he'd been kidnapped by Bison's men in Stockholm and brought here and forced to work for the general. He explained that he was a prisoner, too, and that it was Bison's scientists who'd warped Carlos Blanka's body and mind.

"I did what I could to keep him human," the scientist insisted.

Guile looked down at his friend, still cowering at his feet. "You call this human?"

Dhalsim reached out and tilted Blanka's face up toward them. Guile was shocked to see tears streaming out of the creature's large white eyes.

"His mind retains the capacity for good," Dhalsim said.

Guile glanced back at the misshapen body of the guard lying on the floor.

"Yes, and the capacity for evil, too," Dhalsim allowed.

"Would you kill him because he has difficulty under-standing the difference? Or because he had the mind of a child? Or because he is misshapen? If those are your criteria for execution, when will the killing stop?"

Guile just stared at the horrid creature who had once been his best friend. He had no answers, only anger. Bison would pay dearly for this.

High on the wall next to the bank of video screens, the countdown clock struck 00:00:00. A gong rang, followed by a moment of quiet as the implication of what it meant sank in. Bison turned slowly to his electronics whiz.

"The time has come," he muttered. "Dee Jay, has the AN put the twenty billion in my Swiss bank?"

Dee Jay's fingers sprang over a computer keyboard. Account information flashed onto the screen. Next to the balance was a large, glowing 0. Dee Jay winced slightly and then looked up at his boss.

"No, General," he said solemnly.

Bison nodded slowly. "Then open the hostage chamber."

The massive doors in the middle of the floor parted. The hostages inside squinted up at the sudden light with puzzled, fearful expressions on their faces. Bison maneuvered his floating platform until he hovered over them.

"The world thought very little of you, my dear guests," he said, his voice booming.

The hostages cowered below. Over on the rail, Ryu bristled with anger at the way Bison purposefully terrorized those poor people.

"Yes," the mad general continued scornfully, "the world thought too little to pay the pittance I asked for.

119

Too little even to mount a decent rescue attempt. So you do not deserve the martial dignity of a firing squad. Your masters at the AN called me a wild beast. So be it. You will be killed by a wild beast. A beast born of my own genius!"

Bison turned to Dee Jay and shouted, "Raise the chamber!"

Dee Jay typed the commands, and a hatch in the floor opened. A moment later, the white chamber rose from the laboratory on the floor below. Two rows of razor-sharp knives rose up from the floor to lead the creature toward the hostage pit.

"Behold!" Bison cried. "The face of your destruction . . . and of my victory!"

The doors of the chamber parted. A thick cloud of fog and vapor escaped. The hostages backed away from the light. A fiendish, vicious smile creased Bison's lips. On the catwalk at the back of the room, Ryu's knuckles turned white, and he squeezed the rail in fearful anticipation.

A figure leaped from the chamber. A blur of power and motion, it cleared the fence of knives and headed straight toward Bison!

Whomp! He smashed into Bison feet first, slamming the warlord to the floor of his floating platform. In a flash, he pulled a pistol and jammed it against Bison's head.

"It's Guile!" Chun-Li cried.

Bison's troopers milled around, confused and uncertain of what to do. The hostages stepped back into the light.

"Yahoo!" "All right!" The street fighters cheered happily.

120

On the floating platform, Bison stared up at Guile, stunned. "How is this possible?" he asked, gasping. "I destroyed you. I saw it on my TV."

"Maybe you ought to switch to cable," Guile replied with a smile as he pointed at the bank of video screens. Bison looked up. A huge force of AN troops, led by Captain Sawada, was racing upriver in landing craft!

Guile followed Bison's eyes to other screens, showing his troopers in the fortress going about business as normal. They had not been alerted to the attack. Clearly they had no idea of what was heading toward them.

Bison turned and locked eyes with Dee Jay, sending a silent message. The electronics whiz instantly swiveled his head and locked eyes with an ominous bald technician at the control center, who glanced down at a large red lever marked RED ALERT.

Meanwhile, an incensed Zangief started toward Guile. The colonel cocked his pistol and pressed the barrel against Bison's head. "Now, now," he warned, "I wouldn't try anything rash. Anybody moves and you're all out of work."

Zangief froze, but the bald tech started to inch his way toward the alert lever. Guile caught a glimpse of him in the reflection from Bison's platform and instantly aimed his gun at the man.

"That means you, too, chromedome," Guile ordered. "One more move and you're in the Shadaloo unemployment line."

The bald technician stopped and raised his hands. Guile yanked Bison to his feet, keeping the gun pressed firmly against his head. He moved toward Dee Jay and gestured to the street fighters handcuffed to the catwalk.

"Release those prisoners," Guile ordered.

Dee Jay hesitated and looked at Bison uncertainly.

"Let me rephrase that," Guile said, aiming his pistol at Dee Jay's feet.

Blam! The gun went off, and a bullet ricocheted off the floor near Dee Jay's shoes. In a flash, the electronics whiz dashed up a ladder, digging into his pocket for his keys.

Guile noticed that Bison's attention was elsewhere. Turning back to the giant screen, he saw why. The AN Zodiacs were coming ashore near the ruins. Thus far, not a single Bison trooper had spotted them. But in a few moments, the AN forces would have Bison's stronghold surrounded.

Guile and Bison weren't the only ones watching what was happening outside. So were the troopers in the command center. Some of them tensed and started to raise their rifles.

Guile saw that they were thinking of firing. He yanked Bison around so that they could see clearly the gun pressed against their leader's head. But the troopers kept their guns raised. They still weren't convinced.

Guile put his lips close to Bison's ear. "Usually you never shut up," he said with a growl. "Say something to your troopers that I'll like."

"Don't try to shoot him!" Bison shouted. Then, without warning, he added, *"Shoot the hostages!"*

Seventeen

Blam! Blam! Blam! The troopers started firing into the hostage pit. The terrified hostages cowered around the edges of the pit, trying to protect themselves from the fusillade of bullets.

Dee Jay had just reached the catwalk. But at the sound of gunshots, he quickly spun around to leave.

"Not so fast!" Ryu stuck out his foot to trip him, and the keys went flying. Hanging on to the rail like a ballet dancer, Ken desperately stretched his leg out and bounced the keys off his ankle like a hacky sack.

Jingle . . . jingle. . . . Again and again Ken bounced the keys off his ankle in a superhuman attempt to save them from falling to the floor below. The rest of the street fighters watched in silent awe.

Jingle . . . jangle. . . . Ken reached for one last kick and . . . *missed!*

The keys fell to the floor below. Ken looked sheepishly into the eyes of his fellow street fighters. "Hey," he said with a shrug, "I tried."

"Now *I'll* try," Honda grumbled. "Come on, Balrog."

The two powerhouses grabbed the rail and yanked with all their might.

Sprong! The railing snapped.

"Show-off," Ken muttered.

123

Blam! Blam! Blam! Bison's troopers were still firing at the hostages.

Pang! Zing! Plong! Bullets were hitting the steel walls and ricocheting all over the place.

Guile had no choice. He had to protect the hostages. Flinging Bison away, he dove for the hostage pit control panel and smashed it with one powerful kick.

The massive steel doors started to close. Once again the hostages were trapped in the dark inside, but at least they were safe.

No longer able to shoot at the hostages, Bison's troopers aimed their guns at Guile.

Blam! Blam! Blam! Bullets started to rain down on him. Guile dove behind some rubble left over from the ancient temple.

Ping! Zing! Bullets ricocheted all around him. The air was heavy with the smell of burned gunpowder.

Blam! Blam! Guile fired back. Then he saw the bald tech move toward the RED ALERT lever. Guile quickly aimed his pistol.

Click! Click! The gun was empty!

The technician was just about to reach out for the lever! Once he did, the AN surprise attack would no longer be a surprise!

Guile quickly reached into his belt and pulled out a knife.

Swissshhh! He hurled it through the air.

Plat! The knife hit the tech in the middle of the back. The man's eyes rolled up into his head.

Thunk! He fell forward, landing on the lever anyway.

Briiiiinnnngggg!!! Loud bells and sirens instantly began to wail, alerting Bison troopers everywhere of the attack. Red and yellow lights began to flash.

Guile looked up at the surveillance monitors and felt his face fall. Troopers everywhere in the fortress heard the alarm and were instantly mobilizing!

Meanwhile, seeing that Guile's gun was empty and he'd thrown his knife, Bison's troopers in the command center charged at the colonel. Guile had nothing left to fight with except his body. It was going to be tough going against several dozen highly trained and heavily armed troopers.

Whomp! Wham! Bam! He quickly leveled the first three with vicious low kicks, but the wave of troopers was unstoppable. Suddenly he was surrounded.

It looked bad.

Then Ryu dropped down from the catwalk.

Ken followed, along with Chun-Li, Honda, and Balrog.

Thunk! Ryu wiped out a trooper with a heavy neck chop.

Crack! Ken's fist imploded another trooper's rib cage.

"Nice of you guys to drop in," Guile said with a grin as he smashed a trooper over the head.

"We were wondering what happened to you," Ryu said.

"Yeah, glad you made it," said Ken, banging two troopers' heads together.

"Always happy to join a party," Guile replied as he fought yet another trooper.

"Uh, listen, Colonel," Ryu said as he stomped several more of Bison's men. "You wouldn't happen to have our passports handy, would you?"

"Tell you what," Guile said as he swung a trooper by the arm and threw him into three others. "You get the hostages free, and not only will you get your passports,

I'll personally buy you a first-class ticket home."

"Love to oblige, Colonel," Ryu said, "but it looks to me like you pretty much knocked out the controls for the hostage pit doors."

"You'll have to get down to the lower level," Guile said as he kept fighting. "There should be another set of controls down there."

Ryu and Ken nodded at each other and grinned.

"Maybe they serve caviar and champagne in first class," Ken said.

"Don't bet on it." Ryu winked, and the two street fighters headed for the lower level.

Across the room, Viktor Sagat saw Ryu and Ken leave.

His blood boiled. He had trusted those two, and they had betrayed him. The army attacking outside might bring Bison down. But first Sagat would have his revenge.

The head of the Shadaloo Tong pulled Vega away from the crowd and led him away toward the lower level, following Ryu and Ken.

Meanwhile, Guile fought with one eye on the surveillance monitors on the wall. He saw now that Bison's troopers were pouring out of the fortress and engaging the AN troopers in hand-to-hand combat outside the temple walls.

Another street fighter dropped down beside Guile and began to fight. It was Chun-Li. She and Guile fought back to back, kicking trooper after trooper into next week.

"Colonel Guile, good to see you again," Chun-Li said with a smile as she fought.

"I don't know, Chun-Li," Guile replied. "You show up

in the most unlikely places."

"You *could* thank me for my help," Chun-Li said, only half kidding.

"You really want to help?" Guile asked. "Go down to the lower level with Ryu and Ken and get those hostages out of here and to safety."

"Sorry." Chun-Li shook her head. "I have something else in mind."

"Yeah, I know," Guile said. "You want to kill Bison yourself."

Their conversation was interrupted by a new onslaught of Bison troopers. Chun-Li and Guile beat them back with their hands, feet, and everything else they could use. A few moments later they were standing back to back again, engaged in regular hand-to-hand combat with the enemy.

"You don't understand, Colonel," Chun-Li tried to explain. "Bison killed my father."

"There are sixty-three mothers and fathers locked up below us right now," Guile replied. "You can go on chasing your revenge. Maybe you'll get it. But meanwhile, the world will get a whole new crop of orphans. Is that what you really want?"

Chun-Li had to admit that it wasn't.

"Then go do what I said," Guile said.

"You know, for a soldier, you make a lot of sense," Chun-Li said.

"I'll take that as a compliment," Guile replied.

"And I'll go see what I can do," said Chun-Li.

"Good." Guile paused to roundhouse a trooper in the head, knocking him back into four others.

Chun-Li started away, then hesitated and looked back at Guile. "Colonel—" she began.

"Don't say, 'Be careful,' " Guile said.

Chun-Li smiled. "When you find Bison, make him suffer."

"Count on it," Guile answered.

Eighteen

The fighting outside the temple was at a standoff. The problem was the heavily fortified entrance to the fortress. As the fighting raged, Cammy walked calmly through the battle, looking for a way to get in. She found it in the form of an American-made bazooka dropped by one of Bison's men. The man had been considerate enough to leave behind a shell as well.

With troopers grappling and bodies flying around her, Cammy loaded the shell and aimed it at the fortress door.

Ka-boom! She fired the bazooka, blowing the doors right off their hinges.

Sooweeet! Cammy stuck her fingers in her mouth and whistled.

In the midst of fighting, T. Hawk turned toward the sound and saw Cammy pointing at the gaping opening where the doors had once been.

"How'd you do that!" T. Hawk yelled.

"Borrowed something!" Cammy yelled back, holding up the bazooka. "Care to go in?"

T. Hawk grinned. "Sounds good." He turned and waved to a squad of AN commandos. "Gentlemen, if you'll come this way!"

Dee Jay didn't like bullets. No way. It wasn't in his

contract and it wasn't part of his job. He should have been getting combat pay for this! Ducking down around the computer console, he struggled to get some controls back on-line. At this point he wasn't doing it for General Nut Case. He was doing it for himself. He had to slow down those AN commandos so he could get his act together and blow this joint.

Suddenly a figure dropped down beside him. Oh, no—it was the big, bad wolf himself!

"Dee Jay," Bison cried, "where is Blanka? Where is my genetic warrior?"

If that Blanka dude had any brains left, he was probably out taking a swim down the Shadaloo River, but Dee Jay couldn't say that. Instead he acted real panicked. "I don't know!" he shouted. "Everything's crashing!"

"Find him!" Bison yelled. "Check the security surveillance system!"

Dee Jay hit the controls. The audio came up before the video. Screams of panic, gunfire, groans of pain. Now the visual flickered on. Bison troopers were running this way and that in confused terror.

"What's wrong with them?" Bison asked, gasping.

Dee Jay peered more closely at the screen. Down at the end of a corridor, a shadowy, bestial figure was flinging men around like dolls.

"I have a feeling they met someone they didn't like," he said, pointing at the screen.

Bison peered down. "It's Blanka! He . . . he's fighting my men!" the warlord said with a gasp. "How could he?"

"Man, I think he fights whoever he meets," Dee Jay said. "I knew a guy like that once—"

"No," Bison said. "It's Dhalsim! The cerebral programming. Dee Jay, patch it in here at once!"

The electronics whiz was peeved. This was definitely *overtime!* But Dee Jay had a feeling that this was the wrong time to bring it up. Once again he tapped the keys, pulling up the most recent programming Dhalsim had run through the brainwashing virtual reality chamber.

Images of peace, love, and humanity played across the video screen.

"NOOOOO!" Bison screamed.

Smash! In a livid fury, he smashed his fist into the computer screen. Dee Jay ducked as pieces of the computer went flying. Oddly, Bison grew calm after that. He gazed up at the surveillance screens and saw the AN commandos swarming through the corridors of the fortress.

"Then defeat is a possibility," he said solemnly. "Very well. We shall face it together, Dee Jay. With the stoicism of true warriors."

Bison's eyes were riveted on the action unfolding on the screens above. Meanwhile, Dee Jay quietly backed away. There was no defeat clause written into his contract either. Maybe Bison wanted to go down with the ship, but it was time for Dee Jay to blow this joint and start typing a new resume.

"Dee Jay?" Bison looked around puzzled when he realized his electronics whiz was no longer there.

Dee Jay wasn't the only one making plans to take leave of this madness. Down on the lower level, Ken and Ryu fought their way through a squad of Bison troopers, but as Ryu turned to search for a way to release the hostages, Ken turned toward the exit.

"What are you doing?" Ryu asked during the brief

131

moment of calm.

"Splitting," Ken replied.

"Why?"

Ken couldn't believe how naive his partner could be. "Hey, listen, Ryu, considering the fact that Guile put a gun to our heads and forced us into this mess, I think we've been good little soldiers. But the debt's been paid, okay? Now that the real soldiers are here, I'm gone."

"What's wrong with you?" Ryu asked.

"Wrong?" Ken frowned.

"Yeah. There are people fighting upstairs," Ryu said. "People are dying up there, man. They're not walking away."

"Right," Ken said, "but they're getting paid to fight, get it? Remember how it was on the streets? No pay, no play. We're not getting paid."

"Yeah, we are," Ryu said.

"In what?" Ken asked sourly. "Gratitude dollars?"

Ryu put his hands on his hips and shook his head sadly. It seemed as if his buddy would never understand.

"Hey, look, Mr. Holier-Than-Thou," Ken said, "you coming or not? Maybe if we go now we can find something worthwhile in this place before it blows sky high."

"I already found something worthwhile," Ryu replied.

Ken scowled. "Like what?"

"You wouldn't understand," Ryu said.

The two street fighters stared at each other silently for a moment. But Ryu couldn't waste any more time. There were hostages who needed to be saved.

"See you around." He gave Ken a chilly wave and turned away.

Guile was still fighting Bison's troopers hand-to-hand.

It was an exhausting exercise, and then he suddenly realized three more had snuck up behind him. He wondered if he had the endurance to go the distance with them.

Rumble . . . *!* Just then, the stone wall beside the troopers toppled over, scattering them. As the dust cleared, Guile looked up in surprise. It was Honda, dressed like a sumo and ready to fight!

Arrruuugghhh! Across the room, Zangief let out a roar. The two titans charged each other.

Whomp! In the middle of the command center they collided like freight trains meeting head-on.

Whoops! As they wrestled over the floor hatch leading down to the lab, the hatch gave way under their weight. Guile watched in amazement as the two giants disappeared from sight.

Something tapped him on the arm. Guile spun around, raising his hands to fight. . . .

But it was only Cammy.

"Sorry to startle you, sir," she said, saluting formally.

"It's okay." Guile relaxed. "At ease, Lieutenant. Progress report?"

"Ground level and this floor are secure, sir," Cammy reported. "Sawada's team is working its way deeper into the complex."

"And Bison?" Guile asked.

"No sign of him, sir."

Guile smirked and shook his head wearily. "He's probably hiding."

"Hiding!?" A voice boomed over the room.

Everyone looked up. A huge, live image of Bison, as pompous as ever, filled every one of the video screens.

"What do I have to fear from you?" Bison asked haughtily. "You are mere worker ants, scurrying about

133

with your pitiful weapons, afraid of the purity of unarmed combat."

"Come out from behind the curtain, Wizard," Guile shouted back. "Let's see how pure your combat really is."

Guile started to pull off his battle vest and undo his gun belt.

"Sir, no!" T. Hawk said, gasping. "Don't you see that that's exactly what he wants you do to?"

Bison stepped out from behind the video screens, the real man dwarfed by the video image towering over him.

"No, Hawk." Guile stripped down to the sleeveless blue military T-shirt. "This is what we both want. Am I right, Bison? Are you man enough to fight with me?"

"Anyone who opposes me will be destroyed," Bison announced confidently.

The two men approached each other in the middle of the command center floor.

"Colonel," Cammy said with a gasp. "You can't—"

"Yes, I can." Guile looked back at her. "You just get out of here. If I'm not topside in fifteen minutes, evacuate without me."

Neither Cammy nor T. Hawk moved.

"That's an order!" Guile shouted.

Cammy and T. Hawk glanced at each other and then slowly left the room.

Nineteen

The dust and flying debris made it hard for Chun-Li and Balrog to find their way through the lower level. Bison troopers seemed to come from all directions, only to be met by Chun-Li's devastating kicks and Balrog's monstrous punches.

But just how to free the hostages remained a mystery.

"What happened to Honda?" Balrog asked as they fought side by side.

"I don't know," Chun-Li said. "He was with us, and then I turned around and he was gone."

"Boy, I wish I knew where he was," Balrog said.

Crash! No sooner had the words left Balrog's lips than Honda and Zangief crashed to the floor in front of them!

The two giants rose from the debris with dust and shards falling off their bodies. They instantly went into a clench that would have crushed the bones of any other men.

"My strength is . . . much greater . . . than yours!" Zangief said, grunting.

"It is natural . . . for a sumo wrestler . . . to be . . . the world's strongest!" Honda replied, also with a grunt.

Still grappling, they rolled away down a corridor like a giant wrecking ball of muscular protoplasm.

Balrog and Chun-Li turned to each other in shock.

"Was it my imagination, or were they both smiling?" Chun-Li asked.

"You weren't imagining it," Balrog replied. "Maybe they're both happy to meet someone who can give them a challenge."

They heard footsteps and spun around as three heavily armed Bison troopers ran toward them from another corridor.

"*Ya-chi!*" Chun-Li leaped in the air and delivered a teeth-crushing front kick to one of them.

Whomp! Whomp! Balrog caught the other two with sledgehammer uppercuts to their chins.

Chun-Li grabbed the trooper she'd just kicked and slammed him against the wall. "The hostages!" she screamed. "Where are they?"

The terrified man pointed down the corridor with a trembling finger.

Wonk! Chun-Li gave him a head butt, knocking him cold. Then she and Balrog raced down the hall.

One thing about nuts like Bison, Ken thought as he moved quietly through underground rooms, *they tend to be rich nuts*. Up ahead through an open doorway, he heard the sound of tumblers falling as someone opened a safe. Ken froze and listened. He heard clicks and clacks, and then the soft scraping sound of a strongbox being pulled from a wall safe.

They were sounds Ken knew well. He sprang forward, determined to find the person before he or she got away. But as he entered the small room, he realized the person was gone. The door of the safe was open. Clearly, whatever had been inside had now vanished.

Ken shook his head in disgust. It seemed like you

couldn't trust anyone these days! Then he noticed a gold statue standing nearby. Whoa, wouldn't it be great if it was solid gold? Ken smiled to himself, knowing it couldn't be. No one but a nut would leave a solid gold statue that large just sitting around.

Just for the hell of it, Ken decided to pick it up. His eyes bulged with surprise. The thing weighed a ton! Could it really be? Was Bison *that* crazy? It appeared that he was. Ken hefted the statue up into his arms. Looked like this was his lucky day after all! All he had to do was get this thing out of the country and he was set for life!

But to get out of the country, he first had to get out of Bison's fortress. Ken looked around and spotted a communication console.

"Okay," he said to himself, "this oughta help me find the front door."

He started typing keys, but all that came up on the screen was scene after scene of fighting everywhere. Ken kept skipping to different screens. He almost passed one that showed someone in a white karate outfit.

Whoa! Ken froze. That was Ryu! He looked more closely. The video camera was positioned to watch a point where two converging corridors intersected. Ryu was coming down one corridor. Sagat and Vega were coming down the other! In a second Ryu was going to come face-to-face with them! And that was a face-to-face he wasn't likely to survive!

A microphone jutted out from the console. Ken bent down and spoke into it. "Hey, Ryu, this one's for old times' sake. You're walking right into a trap, *amigo*."

But on the screen, Ryu kept walking. He gave no indication that he'd heard. Ken tapped the mike, then checked the jack.

"Ryu!" he called again. "You clock me?"

Nothing. The audio wasn't getting through. Ken stared at the screen. Every step brought Ryu closer to an extremely unpleasant meeting with Vega and Sagat.

Bison and Guile faced off alone in the command room. Bison had a crazed smile on his face.

"What're you smiling at?" Guile asked.

"You, of course," Bison replied. "You've made me a very happy man."

"I'm glad," Guile shot back. "Because now I'm gonna make you a very dead one!"

Guile launched himself into the air.

Whomp! He hit Bison square in the chest with both feet. The warlord flew backward.

Crash! Bison smashed into a computer panel. Sparks and flames jumped out around him.

As Guile stepped closer, Bison pushed himself off the panel and whirled in the air, kicking high. Guile ducked.

Clank! Bison's armor boot bashed into a bulkhead, denting it.

Wham! Guile jumped and delivered a driving kick to Bison's chest.

"Ugh!" The warlord grunted and staggered backward a few feet, then regained his balance and smiled. "You'll have to do better than that, Guile."

"Okay." Guile did a backflip and caught the warlord in the chin.

Whack! This kick practically took Bison's head off. The warlord staggered backward, stunned.

Crunk! Guile smashed him in the face with his fist. "That's for what you did to Carlos!"

Thwonk! He hit him again. "That's for what you did to his two soldiers!"

Bison was seeing stars. It was a miracle he was even standing. Guile moved in with his fists clenched and a cold smile on his lips. "Just think, Bison, sixty-three more to go."

Ker-pow! With one last humongous, crushing blow, Guile sent Bison flying backward into his floating platform.

Zzzzzzttttt! Bison smashed into the controls, sending sparks in all directions. A great blue web of electricity embraced him, and the warlord twitched and jerked spasmodically as he was electrocuted.

Guile held his breath and watched. He was taking no chances. Finally, the sparks and crackling bolts of electricity faded. Bison slumped backward on the controls. Guile reached out and pressed two fingers against the warlord's neck.

There was no pulse.

The bastard was dead.

Twenty

A wave of relief and fatigue swept through him. Guile reached into his pocket and brought out a small walkie-talkie. "This is Guile. Cammy? T. Hawk? Anyone there?"

A female voice with a British accent crackled back. "Colonel! Cammy here. Are you all right?"

"I'm okay," Guile said. "Just half dead."

"And Bison?" Cammy asked.

"All dead," Guile said. "What's the situation?"

Unseen behind Guile, Bison's sophisticated body armor began to throb as it automatically administered CPR.

"We've encountered fighting in every corridor, sir," Cammy reported via the walkie-talkie. "Resistance is high. It's very slow going."

Bison's body jerked as his armor administered life-restoring jolts to his heart.

"And the hostages?" Guile asked.

"We haven't found them yet, sir, but they continue to be our number-one priority."

"I've got some volunteers working on it, too," Guile said. "Maybe—"

He noticed something out of the corner of his eye and spun around.

"Sir?" Cammy's voice came over the walkie-talkie. "Sir, are you still there?"

Guile couldn't believe what he was seeing. Bison stood before him, as alive as ever, his eyes gleaming with evil. The warlord slowly raised his arms.

"Colonel?" Cammy called.

Guile braced himself. Something bad was coming.

Zzzzzzttttt! Bolts of blue lightning surged out of the metallic gloves covering Bison's clenched fists. Ozone crackled in the air.

Whomp! Guile was knocked off his feet and backward to the floor. Shaking the confusion out of his head, he watched as Bison stepped triumphantly toward him.

"A weapon, Bison?" Guile asked scornfully. "What happened to the purity of unarmed combat?"

Bison stopped and raised his gloves. An electric hum filled the air.

"Weapon?" Bison repeated. "Hardly. This is merely superconductor electromagnetism. Surely you've heard of it. It levitates bullet trains from Tokyo to Osaka."

Bison pointed at his floating platform. "It levitates my desk, where I ride the saddle of the world. And . . . it levitates *me*."

The hum grew louder and the soles of Bison's metal boots began to glow. As Guile watched, astonished, the warlord rose off the floor and shot toward him.

Whomp! Bison delivered a blow that sent Guile reeling backward into a wall. The warlord followed, floating above like an angel of death.

"Something wrong, Colonel?" Bison shouted with mad glee. "Let me guess! You came here prepared to fight a madman . . . and instead, you found a god!"

Bison blasted toward him, preparing to deliver another devastating blow. His cape flapped behind him like Superman's. This time Guile could only wait for the impact, and wonder if he'd finally fought his last fight.

After finding Ryu alone in the corridor, Vega had begged Sagat to let him take on the street fighter alone. Sagat had granted his wish. They fought through the barracks locker room with walls lined with red lockers.

"Let's pick up where we left off," Vega cried, forcing Ryu against a locker. "Now, where were we?"

"You were losing," Ryu replied.

Slash! Vega whipped the fearsome claw around, ripping through Ryu's shirt and leaving thin trails of blood across his chest.

"I think you must be mistaken," Vega said.

"We'll see about that," Ryu spit back.

Vega came in with another slashing movement. This time Ryu ducked, spun and slammed him in the ribs with an elbow.

"Ahhhh!" Vega doubled over in pain.

"Yeah." Ryu smiled. "I thought I was right."

Wham! A sharp, piercing pain radiated from the small of Ryu's back. He turned and saw that Sagat had come up behind him and delivered a blow to his kidney.

"I thought you were going to let Vega fight me alone," Ryu said in surprise.

"Only as long as it looked like he was winning," Sagat replied with an evil grin.

Rip! Ryu felt searing pain rake across his shoulder. Vega had slashed him from behind!

Ryu quickly backflipped, but found himself in a corner. Vega and Sagat were closing in for the kill.

Crack! Sagat suddenly went flying sideways and

142

smashed into a wall of lockers.

Ryu looked up, amazed to find that Ken had delivered the blow. "Ken! What made you come back?"

"Ah . . . I guess I met a dragon," his friend replied with a smile.

"Huh?" Ryu was too distracted by the fight to understand.

"It's chi," Ken explained. "Like Guile said."

"Good timing," Ryu said, gesturing to Vega and Sagat.

"Yeah." Ken looked at Ryu's torn karate suit and then at his own. "Hey, there's just one thing. I want to make sure there's no mistake about whose side we're on."

He reached to his chest and ripped the Bison insignia from the suit.

"Good idea." Ryu ripped his off as well.

"So which one you want?" Ken asked, pointing at Vega and Sagat.

"Well, I started with crab claw here, so I think I'll finish with him," Ryu said.

"Okay, I'll take the one-eyed jack," Ken said.

He squared off against Sagat and they traded blows. Suddenly the tong leader slipped and fell. Ken saw an opportunity to finish him off, but didn't take advantage of it.

"Can't finish the job?" Sagat asked, glaring up at him from the floor.

"Get up," Ken said. "It's too early for you to be defeated."

"You'll regret giving me the opportunity," Sagat said, rising again to his feet.

"I doubt it," Ken said, getting into battle stance.

"Oh, yes," Sagat said, circling him menacingly.

"You've just shown me what you are."

"And what's that?" Ken asked with his fists raised.

"You're not a winner," Sagat said with a nasty grin. "You're a beginner."

The tong leader faked and bobbed. Ken threw a punch that went too high.

Wham! Bam! Sagat delivered a stinging combination, driving Ken to his knees.

Scrack! Vega's stainless-steel claws raked the stone just over Ryu's head, leaving a trail of sparks.

" 'Spanish ninja'? Try *vanished* ninja," Ryu shouted, throwing a whirling kick to the side of his opponent's head.

Sprong! Ryu's foot caught Vega in the temple and his mask went flying. Furious, Vega charged him with his claw held high.

"Handsome fighters never lose!" he screamed.

Snatching the mask from the floor, Ryu used it to block the swiping claw.

Clank! Vega's claw caught in the mask's eyehole. With an aikido move, Ryu twisted both mask and claw away.

"*Ahhhh!*" Vega let out a yelp as his wrist twisted around painfully.

"You've been pretty too long!" Ryu shouted.

Crunk! Ryu smashed Vega square in the face and felt the bones in the cage fighter's nose crumble. Vega slammed backward into a locker. He pressed his hand to his nose and stared down incredulously at the bright red blood. No one had ever drawn blood on him before!

WHAM! Ryu hit him like a pile driver, catching him off guard. Vega crumbled onto the floor. He twitched once and lay unmoving.

"*Ooof!*" "*Ach!*" "*Unh!*" Sagat went flying as Ken deliv-

144

ered a merciless series of combinations. Sagat landed on the floor, with his back against the lockers.

Breathlessly wiping blood from his lips, Ken pointed a finger at him. "Sagat, I owe you. If I hadn't met you, I might have *become* you."

Sagat sat up, feeling his jaw. He knew he'd been defeated in hand-to-hand combat. This was a first. It had never happened before.

And it would never happen again. He reached for an assault rifle left behind by a fleeing Bison trooper.

"Ken, look out!" Ryu shouted.

Ken spun around, but it was too late. Sagat had the rifle in his hands.

Ryu leaped into the air.

Sagat aimed the rifle and started to squeeze the trigger.

Ryu was already sailing toward him, but the distance seemed too great.

"Sho-Ryu-Ken!" Ryu screamed the name of the mystical dragon punch.

Pow! Ryu's fist smashed into Sagat's chest.

Bang! The assault rifle exploded with a flash of light in the tong leader's hands.

Ryu rolled to his feet, ready to continue the fight, but Sagat remained on the floor, his shirt smoldering and blood seeping through a long, searing rip.

Ken walked over and stared down at Sagat, giving him a hard, cold look. "You were right, Sagat," he muttered. "Any coward can pick up a gun."

Twenty-one

All hell had broken loose in the command center. Computer consoles were blowing up left and right, showering everything with cascades of glowing sparks. Electric cables were popping like firecrackers. Warning lights flashed on and off. Half a dozen computer-generated voices joined in a chorus of warnings. *"Superconductor repressors damaged. . . ." "Energy fields unstable. . . ." "Reduce power consumption at once. . . ."*

Neither Guile nor Bison paid attention. They were consumed with the ultimate fight, the battle that would end all battles and pave the way toward the future.

CRASH! Guile ducked as a heavy electronics console flew over his head and smashed into a bank of computers. He'd hit Bison with everything he had, and nothing had fazed the madman. Now Guile was on the defensive. Bleeding, exhausted, every inch of his body aching, he was stalling, buying time while Cammy hopefully found the hostages and led them to safety.

Blam! Another bolt of electricity knocked him backward, sending him sliding across the floor.

"Give up?" Bison shouted.

"Never," Guile muttered, rising unsteadily to his feet.

"Surely you see by now that you can't win," Bison roared, floating above him with his arms crossed in smug satisfaction. "What keeps you going, Guile? What is it you hope to prove?" He sneered. "That 'right' can defeat 'might'?"

The answer was the lives of the hostages, but Guile didn't say it. He had to keep the madman distracted for as long as possible.

"No," Guile replied. "Just that a *hardcase* can defeat a *nutcase*." The insult worked. The dictator turned.

Now!

Guile leaped in the air, kicking upward. But Bison rose a few feet more, and Guile missed.

Thunk! Guile fell back to the floor and crashed in an exhausted heap.

"Haaaaaa!" The control room shook with Bison's demonic laughter.

"You still refuse to accept my godhood?" the warlord's voice echoed off the walls. "Very well, keep your own God. In fact, this might be a good time to pray to Him. Might I suggest an appropriate passage?"

Bison rose up in the room, a dark silhouette against the massive bank of video screens behind him. He held out his arms, spreading his cape like a huge, evil specter. On the floor below, Guile crept backward.

"Try Luke, Chapter Ten, verse Eighteen!" Bison's voice boomed. " 'For I beheld *Satan* as he fell from heaven, *like lightning!*' "

Bison brought his fists together and began to descend, preparing to end Guile's life with one last massive electrical bolt. Guile lurked, backing up against a wall across from the bank of video screens.

Down came Bison through the air, his eyes gleaming, his face contorted in an insane, maniacal grin.

Closer.

And closer. . . .

Guile inched back, his shoulders pressing hard against the wall.

He had one shot left.

His life depended on it. The lives of all the hostages—and of thousands of Shadaloo villagers—all depended on it.

Bison pressed his armored fists down toward Guile's face. Blue electrical waves pulsed through the clenched fingers.

Guile reared back . . . and kicked out with both feet!

Wham! The kick caught Bison totally off guard. Still floating in the air, he had no way of halting his sudden backward flight right into . . .

The bank of video screens!

KRRRASSHHH! Bison sailed backward into the screens, imploding them. The huge videobank lit up like a massive wall of fireworks, glowing and smoking and spraying showers of sparks and glass in all directions.

And at its glowing center, the mighty Bison hung like a moth in a bug zapper and then disappeared from sight.

"Bison," Guile breathed. "You're off the air."

No wall was strong enough to contain the battle between Honda and Zangief. The two giants created pathways of their own through the underground fortress as they smashed each other through steel and stone. Without opening doors, they rolled through room after room like a huge, living wrecking ball. Stumbling into the room where Bison's cherished model of Bisonopolis stood, they slugged their way through it like Godzilla and Ghidra, flattening mountains and squashing buildings.

Suddenly they found themselves outside the hostage chamber. Nearby, Cammy had taken out a set of tools and started to hot-wire a keypad to the chamber door while T. Hawk fought off more of Bison's troopers.

Just then, Balrog and Chun-Li turned the corner and sized up the situation.

"Is this the hostage chamber?" Chun-Li shouted.

"Yes," Cammy replied. "I'm in the process of opening it. This'll only take a minute!"

Smash! Balrog stepped up next to her and drove his fist right through the keypad.

"Actually, maybe less than a minute," Cammy said.

The door slid open. Frightened, wary hostages looked out at the street fighters.

"Come on!" Cammy waved at them. "We're getting you out of here!"

The hostages started out. The street fighters helped them find their way through the maze of corridors. As they filed past Honda and Zangief, the great sumo paused from his fighting.

"Sorry." Honda waved at Zangief and started after the hostages. "I can't play with you anymore."

"Coward!" Zangief shouted, shaking a fist at him. "Come back!"

But Honda disappeared down a corridor. Uncertain what to do, Zangief looked around and noticed that Dee Jay was skulking through the shadows, carrying some sort of wooden box.

"Dee Jay!" Zangief cried anxiously. "Where are you going? The enemies of peace and freedom are at the walls!"

Dee Jay narrowed his eyes in disbelief. "Are you still buying that garbage? When are you gonna wake up and

149

smell the napalm, Zangief? *Our boss* is the enemy of peace and freedom. These people came from all over the world to stop him."

Deep furrows appeared in Zangief's brow. "General Bison is bad guy? If you know this, why did you serve him?"

"Because he paid me a fortune, you moron!" Dee Jay turned and disappeared down a tunnel, leaving Zangief alone in the wreckage.

"You got paid?" he asked in astonishment.

Twenty-two

Warning lights continued to flash, sirens wailed, and bells rang. A din of computer voices warned of a dozen different system failures and the imminent self-destruction of the fortress itself. He should have gotten out of there, but Guile had to make one last stop. His head throbbing and bones aching, he limped into the lab, or what was left of it. The place looked like a bomb had gone off. He'd heard so many explosions in the past few hours, maybe one actually had.

"Charlie?" He made his way through the smoky dark, stepping around the rubble, calling for his friend. "Charlie?"

A huge figure hulked in the shadows. Guile headed toward it.

"Charlie!" he cried. The sight of his friend's mutated form still sent shivers through Guile.

"Go," Blanka muttered.

"You're right," Guile said. "We have to go now. This whole place is going to blow."

"Not me . . . I . . . cannot . . . go . . . out," Blanka muttered in a voice that was half human, half beast. "I . . . cannot . . . go . . . back."

"You can," Guile urged him. "We'll get you help."

"Not . . . like this," Blanka grumbled.

151

"Charlie—" Guile began.

"Leave him," a voice said.

Guile looked into the eyes of Dr. Dhalsim.

"Don't worry," the doctor said reassuringly. "He won't be alone."

"You'll both die if you stay," Guile said.

"Perhaps," Dhalsim said sadly. "But I must atone for my part in this evil."

He reached out lovingly toward Blanka, who cowered at his feet and held his hand like a child.

"You said you did nothing," Guile said.

"If good men do nothing, that is evil enough," replied the doctor. "Go now and live. Live . . . and do something."

The blare of bells and sirens continued around them, but Guile suddenly realized that the computer voices had all blended together into one single warning: *Ten seconds until superconductor meltdown . . . sealing blast door now!*

Everyone heard it. In a small side tunnel, Dee Jay pressed a hidden button in the wall. A wall of rocks parted, and a secret passageway out was revealed.

Clutching the strongbox under his arm, he smiled to himself and said, "Jamaica, here I come."

"I was thinking of Brazil," a voice said behind him.

Dee Jay spun around and came face to face with Sagat. The tong leader grabbed one end of the strongbox.

"You just acquired a partner," Sagat informed him.

"Well, we better run," Dee Jay said, "or you'll soon see an underworld even *you* won't like."

"Nine seconds to meltdown," the computer voices warned. *"Eight seconds . . ."*

Half the hostages had made it through the blast door

152

when the door started to drop. The street fighters rushed to hold it up, but the huge steel door weighed many tons. They struggled to stop it, but their combined strength wasn't enough.

"Seven seconds . . ."

"Honda!" Chun-Li shouted as the sumo came lumbering down the hall. "Hurry! Here!"

Honda hurried under the blast door and added his awesome strength, but even it wasn't enough. The door continued to drop. Soon it would crush anyone who tried to stop it.

"Six seconds . . ."

Zangief appeared and stared at them. Chun-Li gave him a pleading look. But it wasn't until Zangief saw Ken and Ryu that he decided to help. Now he joined the others holding up the door. It was enough! The door stayed up! The hostages got through!

"Five seconds . . ."

As soon as the hostages were out, the street fighters dove for safety.

Whump! The blast door slammed down behind them, sealing off the interior of the fortress.

"Four seconds . . ."

Now that they were outside, Ken and Ryu gave Zangief a curious look.

"Why'd you help us?" Ken asked.

"I took your womens," Zangief explained. "I could not take your lives as well."

"Three seconds . . ."

"Is everyone out?" T. Hawk asked.

Cammy looked around, and an awful thought came to her. "Guile!" she cried.

"Two seconds . . ."

The ground began to shake. The ancient temple began to collapse in on itself. Cammy and the others stared at the massive blast door, hoping for a miracle.

"One second . . ."

"Duck, everyone!" Balrog shouted.

KA-BOOOOOOOOOM!

Twenty-three

A huge explosion shook the earth. Smoke and debris filled the air. Out of the corners of her eyes Cammy saw the blast door blown right off its hinges. Thick black billowing smoke rushed out behind where the door had been.

Then everything became quiet.

The shaken street fighters slowly rose to their feet and stared at the destroyed ruins. The entire temple had crashed down into itself. Only the doorway where the blast doors had been remained standing.

T. Hawk sighed sadly. "There's no way anyone could have survived that."

Cammy felt her tears start to fall. Balrog put a protective arm around Chun-Li, whose shoulders shook with sorrow. Honda stared sadly at the ground. Ken glanced at Ryu and slowly shook his head.

"He was a good man," Ken said.

"The best," said Ryu.

"There will never be another like him," Cammy said with a sniff.

"Damn straight," a voice said.

Everyone spun around.

Just then Guile walked through the smoke and out of the passageway.

"Lieutenant, make a note," he said, stopping beside the utterly shocked Cammy and looking over the group. "Give myself a three-day pass."

"Yes, sir!" Cammy grinned from ear to ear and quickly wiped the tears from her eyes.

"Everyone safe?" Guile asked.

"Everyone, sir," T. Hawk reported with a wide grin. "All the hostages have been accounted for."

"Good work, Sergeant." Guile stepped over to Ken and Ryu. "Well, I guess you've earned your passports back."

Ken and Ryu glanced at each other. Then Ryu turned back to Guile. "You can hold on to them, sir."

Guile looked surprised.

"We saw a lot of things," Ryu started to explain. "We even . . . learned a few things."

"Besides," Ken added, "somebody's gonna have to put this country back together again. Maybe a couple of hustlers can help."

"Ever think of enlisting?" Guile asked.

"*No!*" they both answered emphatically.

Guile smiled and turned to the others. "You did a good job, and I'm proud of you. Thanks to your efforts, this country, and maybe even the world, has been saved."

He turned away. Now Chun-Li came up. "Excuse me, Colonel, how about that interview for my network?"

"Sure." Guile glanced down at her. "But only if you wear that dress."

The other street fighters laughed. Even Cammy had to smile. Chun-Li held out her hand.

Guile shook it.

Not far away, Dee Jay and Sagat staggered out of the

156

secret tunnel into the sunlight. Sagat instantly yanked the box out of Dee Jay's hands and threw it down to the riverbank.

"Hey, I thought we were partners," Dee Jay said.

"Whatever gave you that impression?" Sagat said with a snarl, kneeling down next to the box.

Crack! He smashed it open with a neat chop of his hand and stared in. He blinked, then laughed and stood up.

"On second thought," he said with a chuckle, "it's all yours."

Dee Jay watched the man walk off into the jungle. Boy, it sure looked like he'd shorted a few fuses. But all the better for him! The electronics whiz kneeled down and lifted out a thick handful of dollars. . . .

Bison dollars.

out the Authors

d **Strasser** has written many award-winning nov-
both adults and teenagers. Several of his works
been adapted for the screen, including *Workin' for*
s, A Very Touchy Subject, and *The Accident,* which
ted himself. A former newspaper reporter and
ing copywriter, Strasser worked for several years
vision scriptwriter on such shows as *The Guiding*
ribes, and *Riviera.*

addition to writing, Strasser speaks frequently at
ols about the craft of writing and conducts writing
rkshops for young people. The author of more than
rty novels, Strasser lives with his family in a suburb of
New York City.

Steven E. de Souza, *Street Fighter*'s writer-director,
has many action, science-fiction and fantasy scripts to his
credit, including *Die Hard, Commando, 48 Hours, The*
Running Man, and *The Flintstones.* He has written and
directed *Tales From the Crypt* and has just produced the
new interactive game *Cadillacs & Dinosaurs* for the PC
and Sega System.